Frank McKenzie

Books by Eric Ambler

Dirty Story

Dirty Story

A Further Account of the Life and
Adventures of Arthur Abdel Simpson

Eric Ambler

New York Atheneum

1967

Contents

Part One

Departure from Athens

One

Write it on the walls.

H. Carter Gavin, Her Britannic Majesty's vice-consul in Athens, is a shit.

In my letter I had specifically requested an interview with the Consul-General. But no; I suppose he was off playing golf. I got this H. Carter Gavin instead.

He began by keeping me waiting for half an hour. Then, when I did get shown into his office, he spent five minutes talking on the telephone—some legal fiddle-faddle about a marine damage survey.

He was quite young, not much more than thirty. I was encouraged by that at first. Officials are easier to deal with when they have not been calloused by experience. And when *I* was a boy in England we were taught to look up to our elders and respect them—or pretend to anyway. I thought that at least he would be polite to a man old enough to be his father.

He finished his telephone conversation, hung up, made a note and then turned to deal with me. He was the long-

3

haired, big-head, pompous type—every inch the Branch A, Grade Nine, blue-eyed bastard.

"I'm sorry to have kept you waiting, Mr. Simpson," he said.

It was the *only* polite thing he said. From then on he was absolutely bloody—sneering and sarcastic, like a schoolmaster.

I gave him a smile. "That's all right. No bones broken."

"No bones broken *yet*, Mr. Simpson." He picked a file out of his IN tray and gave me a look. "But if I were you I wouldn't count upon that happy state of affairs continuing."

He was looking at me really nastily. Although I couldn't seriously believe that anyone was going to start any rough stuff in the British Consulate-General, the idea made me uncomfortable for a moment. I laughed.

"No joke, Mr. Simpson." Very cold he was. "Here in these offices you have become quite a celebrated nuisance. But there is a limit to the amount of time we can waste on nuisances. What is it you want?"

"As I explained in my letter to the Consul-General, I want my British passport renewed." I felt that it was time to put him in his place. "I thought your job was helping British subjects. If you find the job a nuisance, perhaps I can talk to somebody who doesn't."

He opened the file. "You are *not* a British subject, Mr. Simpson."

There it was again, the same bloody lie. I took out the wallet with my papers in it. I remained quite calm.

"I have here a British Army birth certificate which

proves my nationality," I said, and prepared to show it to him.

He held up a photostat taken from his file. "I already have a copy."

"Well then."

He read from the certificate. "This states that your name is Arthur Abdel Simpson, that you were born in Cairo, Egypt, on October the sixteenth, nineteen hundred and ten."

"I know what it states."

"It also says that you are the son of Regimental Quartermaster Sergeant Arthur Thomas Simpson of the Army Service Corps and his wife Mrs. Rhita Simpson, whose maiden name is given as Rhita Fahir."

"What of it? My mother was Egyptian."

He put the photostat down. "Quite so. But she was not married to your father."

"That is a despicable lie." I was still calm. "The certificate is signed by the Adjutant of my father's regiment."

"No doubt. Possibly he didn't read what he was signing very carefully." Sneering all the time. "Possibly he didn't read it at all. As Regimental Quartermaster Sergeant your father probably gave him a great many papers to sign."

"My father was an officer and a gentleman," I protested angrily.

"He became an officer certainly." He glanced at the file again. "He was promoted to Lieutenant Quartermaster in nineteen-fifteen. It is possible that he was also a gentleman. But he was not married to your mother."

"The British Army said he was."

He shook his head. "No. In nineteen-seventeen, when your father died . . ."

"He was killed in action."

He looked at the file again. "He died after being run over by a truck outside the officers' mess at the Ismailia base camp."

"He was on active service at the time."

"Don't let's quibble, Mr. Simpson. *How* he died is unimportant. The point is that when your mother applied for her officer's widow's pension it was established that they had not been married."

"Then why did the Army grant the pension?" I really thought I had him there. I'd foxed them before with that one.

He smiled acidly. "When I told you that you were regarded as a nuisance here," he said, "I was making an understatement. A great many other government record offices have been obliged to devote time and energy to your case. The records branch of the War Office was among them."

"So I should imagine."

He ignored that. He had taken up another paper and was reading it thoughtfully, almost as if it fascinated him.

"The British Army is a strange authority in some respects." He shrugged. "Paternalistic is the word, I suppose. It likes to look after its own. It is particularly tolerant and helpful, for example, in the matter of common-law wives. It was helpful in your mother's case, and yours. She got her pension, you were sent to England and given a good grammar-school education. An officers'-family benevolent association paid for your schooling, as you probably know, but the Army made it possible. I doubt if the association was ever told that you were illegitimate."

"They weren't told I was illegitimate because I wasn't!"

"As you please."

"And if I'm not British perhaps you'll tell me how I came to travel to school in England on a British passport."

He glanced at the file again. "You mean the travel document issued in Cairo in nineteen-nineteen? That wasn't a passport. An Army chaplain supplied the necessary information and obtained that document solely in order that you could travel to England and go to school."

"It described me as a British subject."

"Yes it did. I don't suppose the chaplain went into things too thoroughly." He sighed. "In fact, if you had behaved yourself all these years and lived a normal life in England or Egypt or here in Greece or anywhere else, I doubt if the question of your real nationality would ever have arisen. You would always have been regarded as a British subject."

"I *am* a British subject." I decided to pin him down. "What about the passport issued to me in nineteen-twenty-eight?"

"The Army birth certificate got you that. The same is true of the consular renewal you obtained in Cairo five years later and subsequent passports and renewals issued in London and Beirut. It wasn't until your arrest in London in nineteen-fifty-five that questions even began to be asked. All things considered, I'd say you'd been very lucky."

"Lucky!" I laughed.

I had intended to sound as if I had been amused by an insult, but evidently it didn't come out like that. I suppose that bitterness, bloody-mindedness and other things had got mixed in without my being aware of them. He flushed, and for a moment he looked quite vicious. Then he made himself calm down.

"Very shortly," he said at last, "I'm going to have you thrown out of this office. But first, Mr. Simpson, I'm going to make certain you don't come back. To do that I'm going to tell you what is now known about you by me and by every other British consular official in the service who cares to look at your file."

"I'm not interested." But I stayed. How much they really knew might be important.

"I'll start with the Interpol dossier on you."

I didn't like that. An Interpol dossier is nothing but a lot of international police gossip, of course, but if people take it seriously it can cause trouble. I knew that the Athens police didn't have a copy, because at that point I'd given them no reason to ask Interpol for one, and because I still had my Greek Residence Permit. But if this officious young sod decided to show them his copy, things could be awkward for me.

"It goes back quite a long way." He was riffling through it. "And you are variously described as a jour-

nalist, an interpreter, a chauffeur, a waiter, a publisher
and a guide. Which are you now?"

"I am a chauffeur-guide. I own a licensed hire car and
run a tourist service."

He made no comment. "In nineteen-thirty, I see, you
were in the restaurant business in Cairo."

"I managed a restaurant owned by my mother."

"Partly owned by your mother. When she died, you
sold it without telling the other partners in the business.
The buyer charged you with fraud."

"He withdrew the charge."

"Yes, after the police allowed you to regularize the
transaction. The following year you bought a partner-
ship in a small publishing business, also in Cairo."

"Certainly. We distributed foreign magazines and pe-
riodicals. Anything wrong with that?"

"No, but you printed some, too, didn't you? It says
here that your real business was the production of porno-
graphy for the Spanish- and English-speaking markets."

I had also faced this charge before. "That is absolutely
untrue."

"The information was supplied to Interpol in fifty-
four by Scotland Yard. They had quite a lot on you by
then, Mr. Simpson. Is it all untrue?"

"I have edited and sometimes written for a number of
magazines of a literary nature over the years." I knew
this speech by heart. "Sometimes they may have been a
little daring in their approach and have been banned by
censors. Books like *Ulysses* and *Lady Chatterley's Lover*
and *Fanny Hill*, once described by those same censors as

pornographic, are now accepted as literary works of art and published quite openly."

He looked up. "Was *Gents Only* a literary work of art?" He didn't wait for an answer, he was enjoying himself too much. "In January fifty-five you were arrested in London. In your possession were samples of obscene and pornographic material which you had been attempting to sell in bulk. Among the samples were copies of a book called *Gents Only* and a magazine called *Enchantment*. All the material had been produced by your Egyptian company. You were charged, tried and given twelve months. That is when the question of your real nationality first came up. When you had served your sentence the Home Office moved to deport you."

"I fought that deportation order."

"You did, and successfully." He shook his head ruefully. "I don't know how you managed it. The magistrate must have had an off day. Anyway, you were issued a new passport—" he quoted the number—"and then you went back to Egypt."

"Yes."

"Where you proceeded to denounce a perfectly innocent British businessman to the Egyptian authorities as a spy." He was suddenly ugly again.

"No."

"No, what? Are you telling me that you *didn't* denounce Mr. Colby Evans? I have our intelligence report here if you'd like to read it."

"No. I mean that was later."

"Before you applied for Egyptian citizenship or after?"

"I never applied for Egyptian citizenship."

"But you have an Egyptian passport. I can give you the number."

"I got that during the Suez crisis. It wasn't safe to be British in Cairo then. That passport is out of date now."

"Then if you need a passport you'd better go to the U.A.R. Consul and have it brought up to date. Or won't he play either?"

"I am a British citizen, and under the Act of nineteen-forty-eight you can't deprive me of that citizenship, no matter how many other passports I've had." I stared him straight in the eye.

He stared back at me for a moment. "We both can and will." He picked out another paper from the file. I couldn't see what it was because he put it down again immediately on top of the rest. "In December fifty-five a London magistrate gave you the benefit of the doubt. He said you were British. So by way of gratitude to your country you denounce an innocent man as a spy. I suppose that was to show the Egyptians how anti-British you were and to pay us back for those few months you'd had to spend in prison."

"I thought he was a spy."

"Nonsense. Even the Egyptians couldn't make out a case against him, and they tried hard enough. In the end they had to let him go. It was pure spite on your part." His lips tightened. "You're a disgusting creature, Mr. Simpson. Your life is nothing but a long, dirty story."

"I didn't come here to be insulted."

"No, you came here because the Cairo police discovered last year that you had made a false statement in your

application for Egyptian citizenship. You stated falsely
that you had never been to prison or convicted of a criminal offense. When they found that you had, they can-
celed you out. Now, *we*'re canceling you out."

"You can't do it. Under the Act—"

"Under the Act the only way a British subject can lose
his citizenship is by making a formal renunciation of it
on Home Office Form R-Six. In June of fifty-seven you
did just that."

"That is another lie." I was feeling quite sick.

"I have a photo-copy here if you wish to jog your
memory." He leaned forward, shoving it under my nose.
"Why did you do it, Mr. Simpson? I'm curious. A cunning rat like you should have known better. Was it just
another slap at the beastly British, or were you trying to
convince the Egyptian authorities that you really loved
them best?"

I said nothing. I'd signed that bloody form because the
Cairo lawyer who had handled my naturalization papers
for me had advised me to. The British had been kicked
out of Egypt at the time and it hadn't seemed to matter
what I signed. I'd assumed the thing would get lost anyway.

"You don't want to tell me?" He leaned back. "Perhaps you're wondering why we renewed your passport
in nineteen-sixty. That wasn't carelessness, I assure you
—merely chance. While we were out of Egypt the Swiss
acted for us and stored all our records. When we went
back in the spring of fifty-nine it took quite a while to
sort things out. And then your Form R-Six had to go to

the Home Office first for their records. It wasn't circulated to consulates until late sixty. You were lucky
again." He stood up. "But the luck's on our side now.
You're in the black book. It's taken a long time and I'm
sure the dirty story will continue *ad nauseam,* but at least
it won't be a British story."

He closed the file and put it in his OUT tray.

I picked up my wallet and started to leave.

He stopped me.

"Just one more thing, Mr. Simpson. You still have
your old British passport. That is British government
property."

"I've lost it."

He nodded. "I thought you might say that. Well, I'd
better warn you. Don't try to sell it to any of those paper-
fakers down by the docks, and don't try getting it touched
up for your own use. It's been reported to the police as
stolen. Now, you can get out."

Charming, right to the last, the self-righteous prig.

If Mr. H. Carter bloody Gavin reads these words, he
may like to know that he was sending me to what could
very well have been my death.

Morally speaking, he is worse than a shit—he is a *mur-
derer!*

2.

I left the car parked outside the consulate and went to the nearest café for a brandy.

Heights terrify me. Once, on that awful night when I was forced to go up onto the roof of the Topkapi Museum in Istanbul, I was so helpless with vertigo that I felt as if I were falling all the time, even though I wasn't.

That was more or less how I felt as I sat down at the café table—falling, with nothing to stop me but the rocks below. I have always been something of a displaced person; now I was stateless as well.

In ten days' time my Greek Residence and Work Permits were due to expire and I would have to go to the Aliens Bureau to get them renewed. That part was all right; I had kept my nose fairly clean while I was in Greece, and they had renewed my permits for the last two six-month periods. The part that wasn't all right was that when you renewed your permits you *had* to produce your passport, and it *had* to be valid. Last time I had used the old Egyptian passport, which hadn't then expired. I knew that it was no use taking it to what that bastard had called "those paper-fakers." The Aliens Bureau people really look carefully at passports, and the sort of doctoring that might get you past an airport immigration control on a busy day would land you in prison if you tried it on at the Bureau.

I knew where I *could* get a new passport, of course— Panlibhonco. The question was, how did I pay for it?

I'd better explain about Panlibhonco. It is a made-up word used by shipping men when they are talking about "flags of convenience" countries, and it refers collectively to the republics of Panama, Liberia, Honduras and Costa Rica. If you are a big shipowner and you don't happen to like the tax laws or the seamen's-union restrictions or the safety regulations of your own country, you transfer your ships' registrations to one or another of the Panlibhonco states. Then, no more taxes, no more labor problems and your ships are cheaper to run. Quite simple and absolutely legal. It works so well in fact that there are now more merchant ships flying the Liberian flag than there are flying the American or British. Other small countries are getting into the act now. Mr. Aristotle Onassis (a Greek born in Turkey, but with Argentinian citizenship) owns ships sailing under no less than five different flags of convenience.

Of course, it's highly convenient, too, for the Panlibhonco countries themselves. They get fat registration fees and all they have to do for them is issue the registration certificates. They don't have to bother about the ships. They may never even see them. Money for jam.

Which brings me to the gentleman I shall call "Mr. Gomez," though that is nothing like his real name.

A ship's registration certificate is really nothing more than her passport, and Mr. Gomez had the idea that if it

was all right for his government to sell flags of convenience, it was all right for him to sell passports of convenience. As he is a Second Secretary to one of the Panlibhonco legations in Athens he has been able to put this
idea into effect.

The trouble is that his passports are terribly expensive.
He wants forty thousand drachma, cash, take it or leave
it. If you have American money he will come down a
little; you pay twelve hundred dollars. But that's as low as
he'll go. You have to deal through an intermediary, of
course; Mr. Gomez doesn't want you coming to see him
personally at the legation. The intermediary is a man
called Gennadiou, a yacht broker with an office by the
harbor at Tourcolimano. He handles everything. But
Mr. Gomez will sell to you only under two conditions.
The first is not too bad: you can't use the passport in its
country of origin. Well, who wants to go to his stinking
country anyway? But the second condition is hard. You
have to take a passport that is validated for only two
years and franked as unrenewable. Naturally, Mr. Gomez
has to protect himself. When he sells you a passport he
doesn't record the issue officially; so, if you were to turn
up at their consulate in Rome, say, to have the passport
renewed, they'd take the number and find out that it
was a phony. Then he'd be up the creek. Still, twenty
thousand drachma a year just to have a phony passport
is a bit much.

I didn't have *one* thousand at that moment.

True, I had the car; but when I said that I owned it I
was not being one hundred percent accurate. Legally,

the car belonged to a woman named Mrs. Karadontis. She is a widow with a bit of money and she owns four tourist hire cars, all with drivers working on a commission basis. The car I drove was an eight-year-old Plymouth which needed new brake linings. She was very mean about repairs; in fact, the old bitch was mean about everything, including my commission. Although I didn't really think that she would lend me the money I needed, I knew of nobody else whom I could go to for a sum like that. So I just had to pretend that she would lend it.

I am by nature an optimist. I think that if you can pretend that everything is going to be all right, and go ahead doing things just as if you didn't have to worry, your troubles may go away. Mostly they don't go away, I know, and then you're in a worse mess than ever. But I'm used to messes, and when you're desperate what else is there to do but pretend?

I made up my mind to go to Gennadiou that afternoon and order the passport before I saw Mrs. Karadontis about borrowing the money to pay for it.

Business was slack. I had been driving some German tourists, a couple from Hamburg, for the past week, but they were leaving that day and all I had to do was take them to the airport. I bought half a liter of brandy for them as a parting gift—that always makes them generous when it comes to the tipping—and went to the King George Hotel to pick them up.

They weren't very experienced and I was able to fiddle their bill a bit. The parting gift went down well, too. I had nearly seven thousand drachma in my pocket when I drove back from the airport.

I knew it was no use going to see Gennadiou before
four-thirty because his office would be closed for the si-
esta. I went back to my flat.

Nicki, my wife, was off in Romania somewhere on a
three-week tour with the rest of the troupe. She is an
exotic dancer, and if anyone wants to know how it was
that a man my age, still vigorous but admittedly a bit the
worse for wear, came to have a Greek woman twenty
years his junior for a wife, they must ask her. I will say
only this. My first wife, Annette, was an oversexed neu-
rotic who ran off with an Egyptian army officer and
lived, I am sure, to regret it bitterly. She hadn't known
when she was well off. Nicki is different—quieter, very
practical. A man is entitled to seek consolation, and an
attractive woman is entitled to look for protection. I always handled her business affairs for her, and when she
was in a good mood she called me "papa." I may add that
Nicki worked because she *liked* to work, *not* because I
made her do so. I took no commission. She was completely free to come and go as she pleased, and with
whom she pleased. I asked no questions. I have regretted
our enforced separation very deeply.

I went through her things to see if there was anything
I could sell.

There wasn't much. She had taken the stone marten
stole with her and most of the costume jewelry. There
was a charm bracelet with one or two gold pieces on it,
which might fetch a little, but a little wasn't enough just
then, so I decided to wait before I sold it.

I drank a glass or two of wine and then drove to Tour-colimano.

This man Gennadiou doesn't own any yachts himself; he just acts as agent for the various owners on his books, fixes up the charters and, as chandler, handles all the pro-visioning. He paid me a commission once for introducing some Americans who chartered an auxiliary ketch for a cruise around the islands, so I knew him slightly.

His office is on the yacht-harbor quay. There are pho-tographs of yachts on the walls and a ship's bell rings when you open the door. In the back he has storerooms full of canned goods and large stocks of wines and spirits. It's a nice little business. You wouldn't have thought it worth his while to deal in passports as well, but he's that type, greedy. He has a brother in the police and his fin-gers are everywhere—a small, sallow, sharp-eyed man who wears silk shirts and is very sure of himself.

Of course, when he saw me come in, his first thought was that I had a business prospect in tow. His manner changed when he found I hadn't. It changed again when I told him what I wanted. He scowled unpleasantly and started snapping questions.

"Who told you to come to me?"

"A friend."

"What friend?"

"A friend of Mr. Gomez." Actually, I'd heard about the Gomez passports from one of the "paper-fakers." I'd been a bit short of money at the time, and, since my old Egyptian passport was no good to me any more, I'd sold it to this man who would fix it up with a few phony stamps and palm it off on some ignorant seaman. It had been while we'd been arguing over the price that he'd told me about Gomez. He'd wanted to show me the kind of unfair competition he was up against. After that I'd asked one or two other people in the know and found out that Gennadiou was the man to see.

However, there was no point in telling Gennadiou that his involvement in the passport racket was getting to be a matter of common knowledge. That would only make him more difficult. I said nothing more and tried to look tight-lipped and discreet.

He seemed to be satisfied and after a moment or two relaxed a little. He motioned me into one of the store-rooms behind the office and shut the door.

"This passport is for yourself?"

"Yes."

"But why? I thought you were Egyptian."

"I am British, but they are making difficulties, something to do with my father's army registration. It may take months to clarify. I need this passport to tide me over."

I could see that he didn't believe a word of it, but he didn't say so. He probably didn't care.

"You know the price?"

"Yes."

"And the conditions?"

"Yes."

He told me both the price and the conditions anyway to make sure I understood. I said I did.

"Very well. You pay ten thousand drachma in cash

now, the balance in cash on delivery. It will take three days."

"But that is twenty-five-percent deposit. I was told that it would be ten percent and came prepared for that. Now you tell me . . ."

We compromised in the end on twelve and a half percent. I handed over five thousand drachma.

He counted it carefully. "I will need a passport photograph and the particulars to be entered. The passport must show you as a naturalized citizen, you understand, and your other particulars must agree with those on your Residence Permit."

"How many photographs?"

"One will be sufficient."

I had brought some photographs with me. I handed him one print and my Residence Permit. He began copying down the particulars, then stopped.

"It says *here* that you are an Egyptian national," he pointed out.

"I had dual nationality. In fact I am British."

He shrugged. "It says Egyptian, so the passport must show you as formerly Egyptian. That is the rule."

"Very well." I knew that things might be awkward if I ever had to use the new passport in Egypt, but there was nothing I could do about that. Anyway, I had more immediate problems, in particular the problem of getting my hands on thirty-five thousand drachma.

He had finished copying out my particulars, but he didn't give me back the Permit immediately. He had been thinking again.

"Are you planning to go abroad?" he asked.

"No. I plan to renew my Residence Permit. For that you need a valid passport."

I thought that as a Greek national he might not be familiar with the regulations of the Aliens Bureau.

But he was. "You will have to get a Greek visa in this new passport," he said.

"I know." I held out my hand for the Permit, but he went on fingering it. He was still weighing me up. The eyes behind the glasses were very shrewd.

"Business must be good with you," he remarked.

"It's been a fair season."

"Is that your own car you drive?"

It was possible that he already knew the answer to that one, so I didn't lie. "No, it belongs to Mrs. Karadontis."

"She must be very generous."

"Generous?" I laughed.

"If you can save so much money."

I knew what he was fishing for. He wanted to know if I was safe to deal with, to be sure that I hadn't stolen the money. He couldn't afford complications. Neither could I.

"Oh, I didn't save it all," I said; "I had to borrow half of it from Mrs. Karadontis." I grinned at him. "That was why I laughed when you spoke of her generosity. She is charging me eight percent a month interest."

I had made a bad mistake, though I didn't realize it then and neither did he. He believed me. For a small fraction of a second he even smiled. Then it was back to business again.

With a nod he handed me my Residence Permit.

"Three days," he said. "That will be Friday at this time. And," he reminded me firmly, "the whole balance in cash. Thirty-five thousand exactly."

As if I didn't already know.

3.

Mrs. Karadontis has a big apartment near the Athens High Technical School.

Normally I went there twice a week to show her my logbook and accounts and hand over her share of the car's earnings. I always hated going, even when there were no arguments over the accounts. Bad smells don't usually worry me much—a smell is a smell—but Mrs. K's apartment really stank. Of what exactly I don't know; her dead husband, I sometimes used to think. The smell was a bit like that of water in which cut flowers have been left too long, only much worse—sour and sickly.

Mrs. K herself stank of scent, and the two smells would combine into something that stayed with you like a bad dream. She was a thin, dark woman in her sixties. She had hair on her upper lip and a voice like a file. She drank a lot. In the ordinary way I would try to get there as early in the evening as possible so that she could go over the accounts before she got too plastered. It took

twice or three times as long later. She was a rabid royal-
ist, and when she had a few drinks inside her she would
read newspaper articles aloud and denounce the government, then tell you what a wonderful man her dead husband had been and cry a bit, then start on the government again. She could go on for hours. Admittedly you
got a few free drinks to keep her company, but there
were never enough of them to kill your sense of smell.

However, that evening I left it until nine-thirty. The
accounts weren't due again until Thursday and I wanted
her to be as mellow as possible when I tackled her about
the loan.

She was mellow all right. In fact I thought at first that
I'd left it too late and that she wouldn't stop talking long
enough for me to say my piece. The moment I got inside
the door she started waving a copy of the evening paper
Apogevmatini at me and going on about a speech made
by Mr. Markezinis that she said was treason. She didn't
ask me why I'd called. Any audience was better than
none. She was pleased to see me. She read the whole
speech aloud twice. I sipped Metaxa and made appropri-
ate noises.

I had thought over what I would say very carefully.
She was an old fool in lots of ways, but not when it came
to money. She was a demon about that. And she was a
demon about law and order, too. She herself could cheat
on her taxes, of course, because that was *her* money, but
she would get really furious about other people cheating,
on taxes or anything else. If I had told her that I needed
money to buy a false passport she would have yelled blue

murder and probably called the police. So I had had to think up another reason for needing the loan.

Although I was only seven when my father was killed, I still remember him very well and some of the things he used to say. He was an officer and a gentleman, of course, but he was also a regular soldier with a lot of experience in the ranks, as an NCO and as a warrant officer. He was an "old soldier" and he knew how to make the bread fall jam side up, as they say. One of the first things he taught me was, "*Never tell a lie when you can bullshit your way through.*" And there was another of his sayings I've always remembered, "*If you can't keep your nose clean, don't let them see you picking it.*" He was joking, naturally, because he had a keen sense of humor, but there was always a basis of solid good sense in everything he said. When I am up against things I always try to choose a saying of his that fits the situation, and nine times out of ten it gives me an idea for a way out.

In this case the one I remembered was, "*Why hurt your fists on a man's jaw when it's easier to knee him in the balls?*"

At first sight that may seem merely the colloquial expression of a commonplace military maxim—attack where you can inflict the maximum casualties on the enemy at minimum cost to your own forces. But when you look closely, my father's way of putting it is really deeper and more subtle. The choice of a soft spot at which to attack is given, but the need for reliable intelligence on which to base the choice is also implied. It is a *man* you are attacking. If your spies had told you that

the enemy was a woman dressed as a man, your choice of
a soft spot would have to be different. Again, the choice
of weapons is stated but a limitation is implied. You
wouldn't normally try to hit a person in the jaw with
your knee. Thanks to my father I have a lot of the "old
soldier" in me and an instinctive knowledge of tactics.
The trouble is that tactics don't always work.

First I'd had to decide which was Mrs. Karadontis's soft
spot and then find a way to have a go at it. Her really
soft spot, of course, was her dead husband, but I didn't
see how I could use him to get her to lend me money.
Her next softest, I thought, was the fact that she always
needed someone to talk to, and in the end that had given
me an idea.

There was nothing wrong with the idea as such. It was
quite clever really. All I had to do was dream up a
woman relative of mine whose husband had died and left
her stranded in Australia or South America, then borrow
the money to pay her fare back to Athens.

This relative would have to be about the same age as
Mrs. Karadontis, I had decided, and exactly like Mrs.
Karadontis in every other respect except one—no
money. I had gone to a lot of trouble working it out. I
called her Aunt Errina and wrote a long, pleading letter
from her to me. I gave her an address in Australia. I chose
Australia because the air fare from there would cost at
least thirty-five thousand drachma, and because it made
the story easier. Mrs. Karadontis knew that my mother
had been Egyptian but didn't know what kind of Egyptian. So I made Mum an Egyptian-born Greek with this

younger sister, Aunt Errina, who had married an Australian businessman just before World War II. Like Mrs.
Karadontis, Aunt Errina had no children. I was her only
living relative. I made her letter to me really pathetic. I
wanted Mrs. Karadontis to feel when she read it that
Aunt Errina would be eternally grateful to her for lending me the money to pay her fare. If I knew Mrs. K, the
idea of having a grateful Greek-speaking Aunt Errina
around, practically in her power, would go down nicely.

And it did go down, very nicely, when I was finally
able to get the story out and show her the letter. In fact
she became so interested and wanted to know so much
about Aunt Errina that I almost began to believe that the
old girl existed. When we got to the matter of the fare
and my borrowing the money, however, it turned out
that, while I knew Mrs. K very well indeed, I didn't
know her well enough.

It was the word "air" that she pounced on.

"An air passage all the way from Melbourne? Why
must she come by air?"

The frank answer to that would have been that the
airline ticket cost about thirty-five thousand drachma;
but I was in no position to be frank.

"She is destitute, Mrs. Karadontis. She may even be
starving. In fact, reading between the lines of her letter, I
am certain of it. The sooner she is here and in my care,
the better. As her only living relative I feel responsible."

"Nonsense, man. She would not starve on a ship, and it
would be less than half the price. Fifteen thousand
drachma, fourteen perhaps."

"Surely not." I had forgotten that her dead husband had been a shipping agent at the Piraeus.

"Why do you think that tourists travel so much by freighter nowadays?" she demanded. "Because it is cheap and comfortable. Restful, too. After what this poor woman has experienced, five weeks at sea would be a heaven-sent blessing. Who are you to deprive her of it?"

It required no effort on my part to assume a hangdog look.

"At the moment, Mrs. Karadontis, I am in no position to do anything else," I said quietly. "I have no one to turn to but you. If I can't raise this money I don't like to think what will happen to Aunt Errina. I know her. She is like you, proud and sensitive. When I received that letter today my only thought was to get her here as quickly as possible, to let her know that she is not forgotten."

"You can let her know that by cable," she retorted quick as a whip.

"Unless I can hold out some hope to her, Mrs. Karadontis, it might be kinder to do nothing, to let her think perhaps that I am dead."

"Who said you should do nothing? All I am asking is that you do something intelligent for a change. I do not like lending money. My dead husband warned me. When he knew that he was dying . . ." She gave me a belly-ful of her dead husband before she got back to the point, which was that while she wouldn't *lend* me any money, she would *advance* me the cost of the sea passage against seventy-five percent of my commission until I had paid her back.

"But first," she went on, "you must go to Sakkopoulos
and Company and find out about sailings and fares. I
know Mr. Sakkopoulos personally and I will speak to
him too. I will tell him to send the bill to me."

I know when I am beaten. I got away eventually. My
stomach was churning as I drove home. Obviously I
would have to go through the motions with this Mr.
Sakkopoulos and then, a couple of weeks later, write myself another Aunt Errina letter saying that she didn't
want to come after all. That part didn't worry me. What
did worry me was that in a couple of weeks it probably
wouldn't matter *what* I said or did. If I couldn't get my
hands on thirty-five thousand drachma I would simply
be a problem for the Aliens Bureau and the police.

4.

The next three days were awful. I even thought of selling the Plymouth and getting a rental car to work with;
but I found I couldn't do that, as Mrs. K had the Plymouth's registration papers.

Friday came, when I was supposed to pick up the passport at Gennadiou's office. Naturally I didn't go. I knew
I couldn't talk the passport out of him. The thought of it
lying there somewhere in his desk nearly drove me mad.
On Friday night I became so desperate that I toyed with

the idea of breaking in and stealing it. I didn't because I had sense enough to see that, even if I succeeded, he would know that I was responsible, and he is not a forgiving type of man. He is, in fact, quite capable of violence.

On Saturday I took an American couple to Delphi. It was eight in the evening when I got back. I went to the *taverna* near the flat for a drink. They took messages for me—I had their number printed on my business cards—and there was a message from Gennadiou. Please would I telephone him if I returned before nine o'clock, otherwise in the morning. He gave a number where he could be reached. The matter was one of business and urgent.

Urgent or not, I had a brandy while I thought about it.

The reason for the call was, on the face of it, obvious. He wanted to know why I hadn't shown up at his office and he wanted thirty-five thousand drachma, cash, or else.

On the other hand there were the words "please" and "urgent." If all he had wanted to do was crack the whip, a curt reminder of his existence or an order to be in his office on Monday morning would have been sufficient. It was curious, I thought.

I decided to call him. I had my excuse about Friday ready. There would be no immediate trouble.

A woman answered the telephone and there were background noises which sounded like a restaurant. I gave her my name and waited.

As soon as he came on I told him that I had been on a

two-day trip to Delphi and apologized for failing to keep the Friday appointment.

He cut in before I had finished. "That can be discussed later," he said shortly. "Are you available?"

"Available for what?"

"A business discussion. Some associates of Mr. Gomez have need of a person with special knowledge of the city and its facilities for the purpose of making a travel film. I suggested that you might be suitable. Are you interested?"

"Very interested."

"I thought you might be." He sounded almost jovial. "I can promise nothing, of course. They will have to decide for themselves if you are *sympathique*."

He used the French word. Odd, but I didn't comment.

"What do I do?"

"Be at my office at nine-thirty."

"In the morning?"

"No, tonight." He hung up.

One thing was certain—if Gennadiou was doing me any kind of favor he must be doing himself a much bigger one. I would have to watch my step. But, naturally, I was excited. I had had dealings with film people before. The previous year an American company shooting on location at Epidaurus had hired me to drive the camera crew, and I had had six weeks steady work on that job. If the production assistant hadn't been so fussy about checking the time-and-mileage sheets I would have made a good thing out of it.

I had another brandy, then went up to my flat, shaved

and put on a clean shirt. As my father used to say, "*A clean shirt, a crap and a shave make a new man of you.*" If I didn't exactly make myself a new man, I improved a bit on the existing one. I also changed to my other suit, the American drip-dry that I had bought from one of the room service waiters at the Hilton. The coat was too tight around the middle, but if I didn't do the button up it was all right. In Nicki's long mirror I looked reasonably *sympathique*. If I could remember to keep my chin up I would also look reliable.

Gennadiou's office was locked and in darkness when I got there. I waited for him. After a minute or two I noticed that he was sitting at a table in one of the seafood restaurants on the quayside terraces. Sitting with him was a thick-set, powerful-looking man with short, wiry blond hair. He was wearing a blue sports shirt, and even at that distance I could see the golden hairs gleaming on his sunburned forearms. Gennadiou was doing the talking. The blond man was listening but in a bored sort of way. Gennadiou glanced at his watch and finished what he was saying. The blond man nodded and reached for the wine bottle in front of him. Gennadiou got to his feet.

I moved away back to the office entrance so that I wouldn't be seen watching. A moment later Gennadiou appeared on the road and walked toward me.

I expected him to get out his keys and open up the office, but he made no move to do so. He nodded as he came up to me.

"You are on time," he said. "Did you bring the money?"

The question took me so completely by surprise that I began to stammer.

"But I thought . . . well, no, not with me . . . I mean you said a business discussion . . . other parties . . . I didn't think you meant . . ."

I suppose that because *I* knew so well that I didn't have the money I had unconsciously assumed that he must know too. In a sense I was right.

He stopped me with an impatient wave of his hand. "All right, all right. You didn't bring the money. Does that mean you don't have it or only that you didn't bring it?"

I hesitated. I could have postponed the evil moment by lying, but, as he seemed quite calm about it, I thought it might be safer to let him know now, while relations were still businesslike, that there was a hitch in the arrangements. He was looking at me expectantly, almost as if he had meant to give me an opening.

"Well," I said, "as a matter of fact I haven't got all of the money together yet. As I said, I had to go to Delphi, and Mrs. Karadontis . . . well . . ."

He nodded. "Mrs. Karadontis wouldn't lend to you after all."

"Not to the extent that I had understood when I came to you."

He looked at me coldly. "Mrs. Karadontis is well known by reputation, I find. My information is that it is highly improbable that she would even think of lending money."

"She drinks too much. One can never be quite sure where one stands with her."

"But we know where *you* stand," he said unpleasantly. "You knew the terms and you accepted them. I am ready to keep my part of the bargain. As the person responsible to Mr. Gomez, I intend to see that you keep yours. If you don't, I can assure you that you will find the consequences highly disagreeable."

I didn't need his assurance. The consequences were bound to be highly disagreeable in one way or another. My stomach responded to the reminder, however, with a rumble loud enough for him to hear. I cleared my throat to cover the noise.

"I am ready to do anything you suggest," I said.

"Good. My suggestion is that, as you can't borrow the money, you earn it."

"From this film company, you mean?"

"Exactly." He tapped my chest with a very hard finger to make his meaning clearer. "I have contracted with Cine-Taranto S.A. to provide various services while they are here. If you are acceptable to Cine-Taranto, *you* will be one of those services. But you will remain *my* employee. Do I make myself clear?"

"Yes. I do the work, they pay you the money. How much will it be?"

"The amount of your debt. They will need you for three weeks approximately."

"But what about the passport? I can't wait three weeks for that. They won't pay you for my services if the police put me in jail."

"We can discuss that later." He tapped me again on the chest. "The first thing is to find out if you are acceptable. I hope very much, for your sake, that you are." His hand dropped, and he snapped his fingers. "Now, if you are ready."

He turned and began to walk back toward the restaurant. I followed.

"Do you speak French well?" he asked over his shoulder.

"Fairly well."

"That will be in your favor. Cine-Taranto is an international company. Monsieur Goutard, who is personal assistant to the producer, is French. He seems to speak no other language well. Mr. Emil Hayek, the producer and director, speaks several languages, but not Greek. I do not know for certain what his nationality is. Swiss perhaps. His domicile is Swiss. The cameraman and operator are Italian. But it is Monsieur Goutard whom you will be working with. You will meet him first."

Monsieur Goutard was the blond man with the big arms.

He looked up as we approached the table but remained seated when I was introduced to him. His handshake was perfunctory, to my relief; his hands were bone-crushers with little mats of gingery hair on the backs. He nodded to me to sit down.

He had very pale blue eyes, a short neck and flat, leathery cheeks that seemed as muscular as his arms. It was a face used to authority; the mouth was used to ordering punishment and the eyes were used to watching it inflicted. The small half-grin on the thin lips was, I soon realized, permanent; but it was the grin of a trap; the only thing that would amuse him would be somebody else's discomfort. The way he looked me over made me instantly uneasy and I found myself trying to match his grin with a weak, ingratiating one of my own. I have to admit that Goutard scared me from the moment I set eyes on him.

Gennadiou did all the talking at first. To my surprise —and let me be clear about this: it really *was* to my surprise—he almost immediately brought up the fact that I was Nicki's husband. He referred to her as a belly-dancer, of course. Well, she *is* a belly-dancer, but most people don't understand that in Arab countries belly-dancing is not just a night-club tease but a highly respected art. She uses the description "exotic dancer" in order to make that distinction.

I said as much.

Gennadiou leered smugly. "As I told you, Monsieur Goutard, he is an expert on the subject."

Goutard's eyes were still picking me to pieces. "Does it matter much how you call it?" he asked. "If it looks the same and has the same effect on those who watch, words are unimportant."

He was obviously himself a man of deeds; but what kind of deeds? Instinct told me, even then, that in the past they had had little or nothing to do with the film business.

He gulped down the remains of his wine and, to my relief, took his eyes off me and spoke to Gennadiou. "Does he know what is expected of him?"

"Only in a general way. I thought it better if you were

to instruct him personally."

"The chief will do that. He knows what he wants. My job is just to see that he gets it." He stood up. "We'll go out and see him now."

We left the restaurant.

"Do you wish to use my car?" I asked Gennadiou.

"That won't be necessary."

He led the way along the quay and down some steps to the launch he used for ferrying supplies in the harbor. Evidently the services he was providing for Cine-Taranto and its production chief included a yacht.

It was at a mooring on the far side of the harbor opposite the yacht club and proved to be an old sixty-foot motor cruiser with a squat dummy funnel. There was a small gangway and a deck hand ready with a boat hook to steady the launch while we climbed out of it. Goutard led the way aft to a deck area with an awning overhead, a couple of tables and some canvas chairs. There were three men and a brunette sitting there.

Two of the men were at a table playing gin rummy. They merely glanced up as we came in and then went on with their game. They were the Italians, the cameraman and his operator. Beyond them, reclining in long chairs with drinks in their hands, were Emil Hayek and the girl. I found out later that she was his mistress. She looked about sixteen and very innocent, even in the Pucci slacks she was wearing. Both appearances proved to be deceptive.

Hayek was about my age and not unlike me physically —dark, balding, a little paunchy, with a Roman nose and a full, determined mouth. But there the similarity ended. My hair is gray-brown, his was completely black; my movements are always deliberate and well coordinated, his were quick and jerky; my voice is that of an educated Englishman, his was harsh and guttural no matter which language he was using. And he wore jewelry—a gold bracelet, two rings and a gold chain with a St. Christopher medallion around his neck. He had his initials embroidered in gold on his shirt pocket and on the toes of the black slippers he was wearing. He had two gold teeth.

He sat up, but didn't stand, when I was presented to him; and he didn't offer to shake hands. He waved in the direction of the girl.

"My production assistant and technical adviser, Mademoiselle Kaufmann."

I bowed to her. She looked at me over her drink.

Hayek waved us to chairs. A white-coated deck hand appeared and more drinks were ordered.

"I am told, Monsieur Simpson, that your wife is a well-known belly-dancer," Hayek said.

"An exotic dancer, Chief," said Goutard. "He is sensitive on the point."

"I am glad to hear it," said Hayek. His gold teeth flashed. "In the entertainment business, delicacy and good taste are of the utmost importance. I shall hope to have the pleasure of meeting Madame."

"She is on tour with the troupe in Romania at the moment."

"What a pity. However, I understand that you have experience of working with film production units."

"Yes, Monsieur Hayek." He had said enough for me to place him now. Domiciled in Switzerland he might be, but his French accent came from Syria or Lebanon. I was surprised that Gennadiou hadn't spotted it.

"What kind of experience?"

Obviously it was no use telling him the truth. However, I didn't have to; while driving that camera crew around at Epidaurus I had picked up quite a lot through listening to their talk.

"Location mainly," I said. "Local assistant to unit managers, liaison with municipal authorities, organizing crowd work, interpreting for the director when necessary, making myself generally useful."

"What kind of crowds did you organize?"

"Local people, fishermen, villagers." There had in fact been a Greek working with the extras. It had occurred to me at the time that I could have done his job as well, or better.

"We shall not be interested in fishermen or villagers," Hayek said. "This is to be a travel film. But—" he raised a hand high in the air for emphasis—"a travel film of a new kind. We shall show the past in the present," he intoned solemnly, "and the present in the past."

I couldn't make sense of that, so I just looked respectfully intelligent and waited.

He took a hefty swallow of whisky. "The glory that was Greece will live again," he said. "I shall re-create it. And not just with stones and old ruins but with flesh and blood."

He seemed to expect me to make some comment.

"That sounds a very interesting idea, Monsieur Hayek," I said. Then I thought of something better. "Will you be working from a script?"

He smiled, then reached down and picked up a fat leather-bound book which had been lying beside him on the deck. "This is the only script I need," he said; "this and my imagination. The rest I leave to nature."

"And to the flesh and blood," said Mademoiselle Kaufmann with a peculiar smile. They were the first words she had uttered since I had arrived.

Hayek slapped her playfully on the thigh. "In the beginning was the word," he remarked. "You speak English, I believe, Monsieur Simpson."

"I was educated in England, yes."

"Then you must know Lemprière's *Bibliotheca Classica*."

"I can't say that I do." I was getting confused.

"You have, I hope, heard of the Dionysiac orgies."

"Oh yes, of course." The sportier type of tourist is always interested in orgies. The licensed guides do nothing but spout archaeology. I used to give value for money. Some of those old temple rites were really hot stuff.

"Lemprière describes them in detail," said Hayek. "And not only the Dionysiac or Bacchanalian. Orgies seem to have fascinated him. Of course he always wrote in a tone of shocked disapproval, but he gave the details. And what he didn't give we can well imagine. We shall have no difficulty, I am sure, in reconstructing the various scenes faithfully against natural authentic settings.

Are you with me so far?"

"Yes." By then, in fact, I was slightly ahead of him.

"The important thing is," he went on weightily, "to get the right cast together, both dancers and other types. I shall insist on absolute realism, of course, with plenty of close-ups. That means that there will be technical problems to overcome. When a man and a woman are, as Lemprière puts it, 'performing acts of unbelievable depravity' it is not practicable to have two and three takes. The cameras must get it the first time. I say cameras because we shall use more than one to get our coverage. But much depends on a young, experienced and cooperative cast. That is where you come in."

"I see."

"Do you appreciate what is wanted?"

"I think so."

"Can you help in providing it?"

"I'll have to know a little more. It won't be easy."

"If it were easy," Goutard put in crudely, "Monsieur Hayek wouldn't be paying you."

Hayek ignored the interruption. He kept his eyes on me.

"I have to know the terms in which you are thinking," I said. "For instance, how many dancers and how many other persons, and for how long? Where will the locations be? There is also the question of fees."

He dismissed all that with a wave of his braceleted wrist.

"The details can be discussed later," he said. "The important thing is that you recognize the need for quality.

We must create excitement, not a sense of squalor. Your
task is to find attractive couples. They must be talented
and experienced, of course, but they must also be young
and fresh. Nothing old, nothing off the streets. Do you
understand?"

"Yes."

He couldn't have made it plainer. I had joined the blue
film industry.

5.

Later that night I went to see Madame Irma.

She has a very nice house standing in its own grounds
just off the road out to Kifissia. She never has more than
six or seven girls at any one time and changes them every
few months. Her prices are high but everything is very
well arranged. Clients enter and leave by different doors
to avoid embarrassing encounters. The only persons the
client sees are Irma herself, old Kira, the manageress who
takes care of the financial side, and, of course, the lady
of his choice. If it were "quality" Hayek was looking
for, I thought that Irma might help me to find it.

Irma used to pay me a commission on the clients I took
her, so we were on reasonably good terms. I wasn't going
to come right out with the problem, naturally; but I
thought that if I led her into it gradually and let her

think that I was saying more than I had meant to, she would get the idea that there could be more money in it for her than for me if she cooperated. There *would* be, too.

She is, though middle-aged, still quite attractive, if you don't mind them on the plump side. In fact I have heard that one or two of her regular clients still spend their *cinq-à-septs* with her for old times' sake. It may be true; but by one in the morning things are quiet and she is usually in her sitting-room–office, dressed in a smart housecoat, drinking glasses of tea and telling her own fortune with a pack of Tarot cards.

She was not overwhelmingly pleased to see me there without a client in tow; but when I said that I wanted her advice she thawed a bit and offered me a glass of tea.

What I really needed was another brandy, but I accepted the tea.

"Did you know that a new film company has arrived, Madame?" I asked.

"Film companies are always arriving these days." But I could see that she was intrigued. "American?"

"Italian."

"Who are the stars?" She reads all the American fan magazines and knows all the gossip they print.

"There are no stars in the ordinary sense. It is a travel film, but highly original and artistic, with actors and actresses playing decorative parts—temple dancers, nymphs, fauns, ancient gods and goddesses."

She shrugged. She had lost interest. "What is it that you wish my advice about?"

"I have been asked to help find suitable young dancers and others to act these parts. I hoped that you might advise me how best to find and approach such persons."

"Ask your wife. She would know."

"She is in Romania with the troupe."

"The manager of that club where she works when she is here then. He is a theatrical agent too. What is the pig's name? Argyris, yes."

"Mr. Argyris is difficult in matters of business, Madame, as I think you know. Besides, I doubt if he knows the type of *artiste* needed in this particular case."

I had chosen my words carefully. She gave me a sharp look.

"What type is that?"

Again I chose carefully. "They must be able to act very realistically, Madame."

"With or without clothes?" She had the idea now.

"Both with and without."

"Natural or unnatural?"

"Mostly natural."

"A *tsirkoilo!*"

"Something of the sort, perhaps, Madame."

"Disgusting!"

Her indignation was automatic. Private "exhibitions" were not unheard of *chez* Madame Irma and she well knew that I was aware of the fact.

"It will be tastefully done, I understand."

"Not with my girls, it won't."

I refrained from pointing out the ambiguity of that statement.

"No, of course not, Madame."

But she was thinking again now.

"Why do you ask for *my* advice?" she demanded. "Why did you not go to The Laundrywoman?"

This was Irma's way of referring to her main competitor, a madame who was believed to have a personal weakness for underwear fetishists. My relations with The Laundrywoman were not cordial at that time, owing to a dispute over some commission due to me.

"For a simple reason, Madame," I answered. "This film company is a competent organization with high artistic standards and substantial sums to spend in order to achieve them. They will accept only the most superior talent. So it is to you I turn for advice."

She thought some more and then began laying out her Tarot cards on the coffee table in front of her. "You say substantial sums. How substantial?"

"Three thousand drachma a day each for actresses in the superior category. Six would be required for varying periods. On an average, five days each."

"That is starvation pay. I have to think of my girls. They are all saving for their dowries. Five thousand would be a minimum. Not that I am even considering this infamous proposal."

"Terms can always be negotiated."

She laid out some more cards in a circle. "You say that they would be wanted by the day. You do not mean night?"

"No, by the day."

"Ah, in a studio."

"No, on location. In old temples. As I said, it is to be artistic."

"In the open air!"

"Yes."

"That is truly vicious." She seemed impressed. More cards, more thought. "And what would happen to this film?"

"It will be processed abroad for distribution in other countries."

"Not here? I have friendly relations with the police you understand, but . . ."

"No, not here. The company is particularly anxious to avoid trouble with the police. They are very careful and discreet."

"They had better be." She fanned out the cards still in her hand and shoved them toward me. "Take a card."

I took one and without looking at it she placed it face downward in the center of the circle.

"There will be the male actors to be considered," she remarked.

"I was about to ask your advice on that matter, too, Madame. There is a stipulation that they be fair-haired."

"Some of the best are dark."

"Perhaps they could wear wigs." It was a stupid thing to say, but it had been a long day and I was tired.

She frowned at me impatiently. "Either you are joking —and I do not like jokes about such matters—or you have no imagination."

"I'm sorry, Madame. I wasn't thinking."

"And I do not like to do business with persons who do not think."

I decided that it was better to say nothing. She began to flip over the cards she had already set out and replace them with others, her fingers moving quickly and deftly as she arranged the second circle. Lastly she turned over the card I had drawn. She tapped it significantly.

It showed a man suspended by one ankle from a gallows beam resting on two high tree stumps. Underneath were the words LE PENDU.

"The Hanging Man," she said; "protected by the Knight of Pentacles but within the Lesser Arcana. If you have in mind any sort of treachery toward one who has occasion to trust you, beware. The next card to the Knight of Wands is the one we do not name."

She pushed the unnameable card across the table so that I could see it for myself.

It showed a male skeleton with a death's-head and an oar in its hands ferrying something that looked like a boatload of coffins.

"I tell you this only for your own good," Madame Irma said blandly. "I do not guide the cards, they have their own way of searching the human heart."

I nodded. I had the message.

My sympathies were with the Hanging Man tied upside down to his gallows. I knew exactly how he felt.

6.

It wasn't I who betrayed Madame Irma, but Madame Irma who betrayed *me!*

All right, I must try to be fair. I can't entirely blame the old bitch for the misunderstanding that occurred. The fault was Hayek's. He should never have employed a dangerous thug like Goutard.

Goutard knew absolutely nothing about film production; that much soon became apparent. He was really Hayek's bodyguard, fixer and dirty-work specialist. One sees that a man like Hayek would feel the need for that sort of handyman, of course, but why he should have chosen Goutard beats me. I suppose the fact that Goutard had once been a French paratroop sergeant had something to do with it; a man from Hayek's part of the world would be impressed by that. It may also have been that he'd found Goutard down and out in Damascus or Beirut and picked him up cheap. If so, it was an expensive bargain for everyone concerned, and especially for me.

I had realized from the start, of course, that all that talk of Hayek's about shooting in ancient ruins was eyewash. He had taken out an official permit to film the usual things like the Acropolis and the Temple of Zeus, but that was just a cover. Even if the Ministry of Public

Works had allowed him to use their precious archaeological monuments as backgrounds for the kind of goings-on he had in mind, the thing would have been impossible. I mean you can't photograph fornicating nymphs and fauns with a lot of gawping tourists looking on. You need an intimate atmosphere and privacy.

Hayek's production schedule was simple. For three days he made a show of shooting the ordinary travelogue stuff, but without film in the cameras. After that we went on location by yacht, with the cast, camera crew and some props, to a pretty little bay along the coast which couldn't be reached by road.

The props consisted mainly of three "broken" columns which Gennadiou had had made up in Athens out of lath and plaster. They were only a few feet high and quite light, but when they were set up on a rocky ledge above the beach they made it look exactly like an old temple site. There were also a couple of papier-maché urns for set-dressing.

Not that the set needed much dressing when the nymphs and fauns got to work.

That was where Mademoiselle Kaufmann came in. Hayek had said that she was his technical adviser. I hadn't taken that seriously until the day they started on the orgy sequences, and La Kaufmann, looking as if butter wouldn't melt in her mouth, began suggesting things the girls might do together. Some of her suggestions made even me blush. She didn't seem so interested in what the men did, I noticed. That was Hayek's department.

Personally, I found it all rather tiring after a while. I mean, enough is enough.

I wasn't there when the row started.

Once I had delivered the cast and seen that the financial agreements were being honored daily, there seemed no need for me to be there all the time; and, as Gennadiou had kept well out of the way since the actual shooting had started, I saw no reason why I shouldn't do business as usual with the car. After all, I still had to make enough money to live on, and Nicki wasn't going to be back for a month. And I had a responsibility to Mrs. Karadontis, too.

Frankly, I don't think it would have made much difference if I had known what had been going on. I couldn't have stopped Goutard. I don't think I would even have tried.

On the afternoon of what was to be my last day in Athens I drove some Americans up to Mount Parnes. They stayed there for an hour or so drinking in the bar of the hotel and it was dark when I dropped them back at the Hotel Grande Bretagne. I debated whether or not to wait for an airport job. In the end I decided against waiting and drove back to my flat. Luckily I made a further decision on the way there—to stop in the *taverna* for a drink before I went up to the flat.

There was a message for me from Gennadiou—*Telephone at once emergency*, and his office number.

He answered on the first ring and didn't waste time on politeness.

"Where are you? The *taverna*?"

"Yes."

"Leave and come straight to my office."

"I . . ."

"Don't argue. There is no time. My office immediately. But leave your car by the club. It must not be seen near the office. You understand?"

"But . . ."

"At once, do you hear me? For your own sake, hurry."

He hung up.

There had been fear in his voice. That alone scared me. I swallowed my drink and left without sitting down again.

What I especially didn't like was his instruction not to leave the car near his office. It meant that association with me spelled some sort of risk or unpleasantness for him. And yet for my sake, or so he said, he wanted to see me. For a moment I wondered whether, for my own sake, it might be better to ignore the summons. Then I was in the car and driving out to Tourcolimano.

His front office was in darkness but he opened the door the moment I knocked. There was a light on in the storeroom beyond.

"Where did you leave your car?" he asked. He spoke in a whisper.

"Where you told me."

"Very well. Come in." He shut the door, locked it and led the way back into the storeroom. When he came into the light I saw that he was sweating.

"Where have you been the last two days?" he demanded.

"Working."

"You were supposed to be working for me."

"There is nothing more for me to do there. Hayek is satisfied. Everything is all right."

"Everything is *not* all right."

"Goutard said it was."

"Goutard!" He said the name as if it were an oath. "You ought to have been there to stop him."

"Why, what has he done?"

"He attempted to corrupt the girls."

"To *corrupt* them!" It was such a ridiculous notion that I began to chuckle.

Gennadiou hit me across the face savagely with the back of his hand. The blow almost knocked my glasses off and made my head sing. I put my hand to my mouth and stared at him.

"Perhaps," he snarled, "you will not find it so amusing when I tell you that tonight the police have a warrant out for your arrest." He had stopped whispering.

"*My* arrest!"

"Yours and Goutard's. You were both denounced by a woman named Irma Zygouris."

"Madame Irma? I don't believe it."

"You had better believe it. My information is reliable, I assure you."

I remembered then that he had a brother in the police; but still I could not accept it.

"Madame Irma would never . . . I mean she couldn't do that."

"You deceive yourself. She has good friends in the Commissariat, and two of the girls are named as witnesses. The charge is that you attempted to recruit these girls into prostitution."

"But that is absurd. They already were in prostitution."

"Try proving it. And if you do prove it, what then? You are still a procurer, a pimp. Be realistic. The fact is that Goutard made proposals to them and they told your Madame Irma."

"What proposals?"

He shrugged impatiently. "Apparently he proposed to set them up in a house of their own. A cooperative venture, he called it—some such nonsense. What does it matter?"

It mattered to me. Madame Irma would never forgive that, or forget it.

"The point is," he was saying, "that, while Mr. Hayek is seriously annoyed by the delay and inconvenience this will cause him, he recognizes that the damage has been done. Now we must act quickly to repair it."

"What's happened to Goutard?"

"He is hidden on the boat. But that won't be for long. It is too dangerous. Mr. Hayek has decided that you must both be smuggled out of here."

"Mr. Hayek has decided! That's very good of him." I was over the first shock now and beginning to get angry.

"Would you rather go to prison and be deported officially later? Don't be a fool. Mr. Hayek and I are your only hope."

He was trying now to sound down-to-earth and businesslike, but he was still sweating and I knew what was going on in his mind. Madame Irma had denounced me and Goutard, but she hadn't said anything to the police about Hayek and his film unit. If I were arrested I would be interrogated, and then everything would come out, including Gennadiou's own part in the affair. Then *he* would be up the creek as well. No wonder he wanted to get rid of me.

He had gone into the front office, leaving me standing there staring at a case of canned beef stew and wishing there was somewhere I could sit down. Now he came back. He had an envelope in his hand. He held it up.

"Your new passport, with Greek entry and exit visas, plus two hundred dollars American and passage on a ship sailing early tomorrow morning for Port Said. You'll both be put on board later tonight." He tried to look stern. "When one considers the trouble you have caused him, Mr. Hayek is being very generous."

"It was Goutard who caused the trouble, not me."

"You can argue with him about that on the voyage."

"But I can't just leave." I couldn't seem to think straight, and, although I tried to control it, my voice was getting shrill. "There's my flat and the car—and my wife and my clothes. I can't just go."

"Would you sooner be picked up by the police? They have two men waiting for you at your home now. As for your wife, you said that she's in Romania. You can send her a postcard from Port Said." He held out the envelope. "Here, take it."

I took it.

"Now open it. Come on." He snapped his fingers.

"Make sure that everything is there as stated. Count the money, check the passport. I don't want you making any more trouble."

Everything was there as stated. I made no more trouble.

7.

At eleven Gennadiou took me out to the Hayek yacht in his launch. Neither Hayek nor any of the other film people showed themselves. Gennadiou told me to stay where I was. He climbed aboard the yacht, spoke briefly to the deck hand and then went below. He reappeared a minute or two later with Goutard, who was wearing a hat and carrying a suitcase. Goutard grinned at me as he got down into the launch, but said nothing. The deck hand followed him and took over the controls. Gennadiou stayed behind on the yacht. He wanted no more to do with us.

The deck hand opened the throttle wide and headed for the harbor mouth. Tourcolimano is really the old fishing-boat harbor of the Piraeus and is separated from the deep-water port and dock areas only by a mole. Within minutes we had rounded the mole and were running in on a black, greasy swell toward the lights of the Piraeus.

The S.S. *Wolvertem*, port of registration Monrovia, was anchored about a hundred yards from one of the oiling piers. She was a rusty old freighter with a tall funnel and superstructure amidships. Thickets of samson posts and cargo booms sprouted from the well decks fore and aft. There was a lowered gangway with a light over it on one side, but that, it seemed, was too public for us; the launch swung around under the stern, slowed and then came alongside below an open lower-deck port. A stream of water poured from a drain hole in the plating a few feet away, and the deck hand in the launch swore as he maneuvered to keep clear of it. A dim light came from above, and a hum of machinery. A face peered down at us.

Goutard stood up and grasped his suitcase. His chest came level with the coaming. He slung the suitcase over the coaming, then sprang up after it. I tried to follow but the launch was bobbing about so much that I couldn't do it at first. On my third attempt two hands reached down and grasped my arms. I was hauled on board.

The owner of the hands wore a dirty boiler suit and he didn't trouble to help me to my feet. The moment I reached the deck he began swinging in the two heavy doors which closed the port and levering the securing clips into place. The launch had already left.

Goutard was lighting a cigarette. Not a word had been said. When the man in the boiler suit had finished with the doors he motioned to us to follow him. He was a balding and broad-shouldered man with tufts of curly gray hair sticking out above his ears. He led us forward

along an alleyway, then up three iron ladders to another
alleyway. We were in the superstructure now and there
was worn linoleum underfoot. We passed a door from
behind which there came the sound of a radio; but we
saw no other member of the crew. Our guide paused by
another door, pointed to it and for the first time spoke.

"*Lavabo,*" he said.

We nodded. He went on, then stopped by a third door
and opened it.

"*Cabine,*" he said.

We crowded inside. There were two bunks, an upper
and a lower, a minuscule washbasin, and, on the bulkhead
opposite the bunks, two shelves, a hinged stool and some
clothes hooks. There was a ventilator but no porthole. It
was smaller than any jail cell I have ever been in. Instant
claustrophobia was guaranteed.

Boiler-suit said his final word from the doorway.

"*Il faut absolument que vous resterez ici jusqu'au
départ. Entendu?*" He spoke French like a German.

Goutard nodded. "*D'accord.*"

The door closed. Goutard reached past me and locked
it.

For a moment or two we stared bleakly at each other.
Then, with a shrug, he picked up his suitcase, slung it
onto the upper bunk, clicked open the locks and raised
the lid.

He took out a bottle of brandy.

8.

I awoke at five in the morning. We were moving, and
the cabin fittings had begun to rattle from the vibration
of the engines. In my bunk it felt and sounded as if the
whole ship were held together not by rivets but by nuts
and bolts which had been tightened by hand.

I had a splitting headache, the result either of the
brandy I had drunk or of the lack of air, or of both.
Goutard in the upper bunk was snoring. I tried to get to
sleep again, but it was no good. I had begun to face the
future.

All I possessed in the world, except for my socks and
shoes, was hanging before my eyes and swaying slightly
on the hook. So was I in a manner of speaking—swaying
slightly on a hook.

For various technical reasons too absurd for me to go
into now, Egypt is a country in which I am no longer
persona grata. Absolute nonsense, of course, because I
was born there. Still, I have to accept it. While I might
safely remain ashore in Port Said long enough to buy a
toothbrush and a change of underwear, or, stretching it,
long enough to get a passage on and transfer to another
ship, any prolonged stay on Egyptian soil would be
highly inadvisable. The Egyptian police have their noses

everywhere. Registering at a hotel, for example, even for one night, would be far too risky. In Port Said I could only be a passenger in transit.

But in transit to where? That was what was worrying me.

It had to be somewhere handy. Beirut would have been my first choice; but I'd had a little trouble there before I'd left to go to Athens and the Lebanese are great ones for raking up the past. Turkey, perhaps; but I wasn't too popular there either in spite of the way I'd always cooperated with the police in Istanbul. Israel would only accept me as a tourist. With Italy and France it would be the same story. Syria was part of the United Arab Republic—i.e., Egypt—so *that* was out. That left Cyprus, Libya, Albania and Yugoslavia. Well, thank you very much.

The truth is that, in most civilized countries nowadays, about the only foreigners who are really welcome are tourists, businessmen who want to buy or invest, technicians whose brains can be picked and Americans with aid appropriations to dole out. Soldiers of fortune with my sort of know-how are simply not wanted. The good old liberal principle of live and let live is on the scrap heap. They only want people who can be exploited. If you aren't a sucker you can't come in.

The engine-room telegraph rang and the fixtures stopped rattling for a minute or two. They were probably dropping the pilot. Then the racket started again.

I tried to go on thinking about the future, but it was no good. I began to wonder whether or not I *had* a fu-

ture, whether it wouldn't be better to wait until night
came again, then slip quietly over the side and let the sea
take me.

"Old soldiers never die, they only fade away."

Bull! They die all right. And so do old soldiers of fortune. So why wait for the crab to come and get you?
Why not get it over with yourself, in your own time and
in your own way? You don't need an entry permit for
the sea.

Do I hear mutterings about self-pity? Or moral cowardice? Or even "sin"?

More bull! When you've been up the creek as far as I
have, those words don't mean a thing.

Lying there in my bunk that morning as the *Wolvertem* chugged out into the Mediterranean, I fully intended
to kill myself before we reached Port Said. Why didn't I
do so? I know what the holier-than-thous, the headmas-
ter types, will answer—"a triumph, my dear Simpson, of
physical cowardice over the moral variety." You can't
win with those sods and I don't try any more. Personally
I think that it was something quite different that made
me change my mind.

I think that before we reached Port Said the soldier of
fortune had begun to sense that he was on his way to war
again.

Part Two

Passage to Djibouti

One

We waited until ten before emerging from the cabin.

I had had great difficulty in persuading Goutard to lend me his razor. It was only when he realized that if I looked too scruffy it would reflect on him when we encountered the ship's officers, that he gave in. Reluctantly, though; and when I returned the razor, after rinsing it thoroughly, he rinsed it all over again. You would have thought I had anthrax or something. But the idea that we ought to make as good an impression as possible had evidently sunk in, because he gave me an old short-sleeved shirt to wear instead of my own, which was filthy from the scramble into the entry port.

We found a small dining saloon on the deck above and a colored steward who brought us some coffee and toast. He spoke French. Goutard said he was Senegalese. An officer came in while we were eating. He was a young fellow, skinny and pasty-faced, but tough-looking. He nodded to us and sat down at the other end of the table. The steward brought him coffee and fruit. When the steward had gone the officer looked at us again.

"You're the new passengers, I take it," he remarked in French.

Goutard nodded. "Do you often carry passengers?"

"Not often. It's up to the skipper." He used the word *patron* and grinned as he said it. "If he feels like doing someone a favor. You're the only ones this trip, so far."

"So far?"

"We sometimes ship a few deck passengers at Aden. Arabs. Aden to Zanzibar. They stink the ship out."

"We won't do that."

"No." He grinned again. "But, if you don't mind my telling you, you're sitting at the skipper's end of the table."

"Thanks," Goutard said shortly. He didn't like being told anything. I started to get up.

The young officer waved his hand. "Don't trouble yourself now. That's the only formality we observe on the *Wolvertem*. Everyone, including the skipper, is very relaxed. We have need to be."

Clearly, he liked to talk.

It seemed that the S.S. *Wolvertem*, though of Liberian registry, was owned by a Belgian company. The officers were Belgian and German, the crew Senegalese with some Algerians. She was on her way now from Antwerp to Lourenço Marques in Portuguese East Africa with a cargo of structural-steel sections and reinforcing rods. At least it was hoped that she was on her way. Condenser trouble had forced them to put into the Piraeus for repairs and delayed them two weeks already. It could happen again. Delays, according to Third Officer Bergier, were a familiar story to the men of the *Wolvertem*.

At lunch we saw the Captain. He was a gray, angular man with a narrow head, a bitter mouth and heavily lidded eyes. His name was Van Bunnen and he was Flemish. I judged him to be in his fifties. If, as seemed likely, command of the *Wolvertem* represented the high point of his seagoing career, he had reason to look bitter.

He ignored us completely at first. Since he had taken a substantial bribe from Gennadiou, or some agent of Gennadiou's, to look the other way while we came aboard like stowaways, this was understandable. Obviously he would prefer to ignore the evidence of his own venality. The other officers at the table, including the German chief engineer who had welcomed us aboard and the young deck officer who had talked so freely earlier, took their cue from him. Presumably they also took their share of the perks.

If Goutard disliked being told things, he disliked even more being ignored. His rat-trap smile became harder as the meal progressed. When the coffee came he could contain himself no longer. He rose and walked over to the Captain.

"Yves Goutard, Skipper," he said. "Enchanted to make your acquaintance."

The Captain looked dumfounded for a moment, then rather weakly took the hand extended to him.

"Van Bunnen," he said.

Goutard indicated me. "And that is my friend Monsieur Simpson."

The Captain and I mumbled acknowledgment of each other.

"We hope very much," Goutard went on firmly, "that the unconventional manner of our arrival on board will not be misunderstood. We journalists, you must realize, sometimes uncover information—about little scandals, let us say—that the politicians would rather suppress. In those circumstances we are obliged to move in unconventional ways."

"Yes, yes, of course," said the Captain. Whether he really believed this nonsense or not is hard to say; but at that moment it was clearly more convenient for him to behave as if he believed. In that way we were less of a reproach. He proceeded to introduce his officers.

That was Wednesday. We were due in Port Said late Friday. By Thursday night Goutard and the Captain were as thick as thieves. I didn't care. It suited me to be left alone. I was endeavoring to convince myself that to-morrow would never come and that I need not think about the future.

It was a warm night and I didn't want to sleep in that stifling cabin. I was dozing in a deck chair when Goutard joined me. He dragged a chair alongside mine.

He had been having a session with the Captain and smelled strongly of Dutch gin. He was drunk, but only slightly. His speech was quite clear; he was just a bit more affable than usual.

"You know our skipper's trouble?" he began.

"Too much gin?"

"Yes, but that's not his trouble. The trouble is that he

can't hold it. I left him flat out." His teeth gleamed in the darkness.

"I wouldn't mind being flat out myself."

"There's still some brandy down in the cabin. Do you want to get it?"

"All right."

"Don't forget the tooth glasses."

He was the kind of man who always had to have some-one to fetch and carry for him.

When I came back he was leaning on the rail looking at the wake of the ship. He took the bottle from me, drained it into the glasses and then flung the empty over-board.

"To your health," he said.

"To yours." I sat down again wishing he would go away. I didn't want to talk or think, just make the brandy last. He returned to the chair beside me, stretched out and put his feet up on the lower rail.

"Do you plan to stay in Port Said?" he asked.

"No longer than I have to."

"Where will you go then?"

"Cyprus possibly."

"Whatever for?"

"It's a place."

"Aren't you afraid of extradition? They're hand in glove with the Greeks there."

"I doubt if the Greeks would go to the trouble." It was an aspect of Cyprus which I hadn't considered, though. I wished even more fervently that he would go away.

"Me, I wouldn't risk it. Besides, what is there for you in Cyprus?"

A question to which I had no answer. I muttered something.

"You know where this boat's going, this place Lourenço Marques?" he asked. "Have you ever been there?"

"No, I haven't."

"The skipper was telling me about it. It's in Portuguese Mozambique. That's still a white man's country and no nonsense. They know how to deal with the *macaques* there."

Macaque means "monkey," but it also means "nigger" or "wog" when a man like Goutard is using it. When I was at school in England I used to be called "wog" because I had been born in Egypt. I am not really dark, so I hadn't minded much. But I had minded a little. Goutard had a nasty way of making me remember the things I try to forget.

I said nothing.

"Ninety-nine percent *macaques*," he went on; "one percent white, but it's that one percent that counts. The skipper said he thought I could get a visa from the Portuguese Consul in Port Said."

That shook me. "You mean to go there?"

"I'm thinking of it."

"But all that way?"

"It's only seventeen days or so. The skipper says that if I sign on as assistant purser he'll give me passage there for a hundred and twenty-five dollars."

"But what would you do there?"

"I'd find something soon enough. I know how to deal with *macaques*. I could make myself useful."

"But what about the language? Can you speak Portuguese?"

"I know some Spanish. I'd soon learn. Besides, he says they speak a bit of everything there. They have another big city, too, a place called Beira. That's the port for Rhodesia. I'll bet a lot of them speak English. You'd be all right."

"Me?"

"What have you got to lose?"

I tried to think of something I had to lose, apart from life and liberty.

"There's my wife," I said at last.

His grin widened. "I saw a photograph of her. Very interesting. Were you counting on her joining you in Cyprus?"

I hadn't been counting on anything. In fact, I hadn't given much thought to Nicki. About her, at least, I had no illusions. If I were not there when she returned, she would go her own way. Someone else would soon take my place.

"Why does he want you to sign on as assistant purser?" I asked.

"So that he doesn't have to pay passenger dues through the canal. Maybe he'd make you an assistant purser too. Do you want me to ask him? He likes me."

"When do you have to decide?"

"Tomorrow, before we get into port. But I've pretty

well made up my mind. No more Hayeks for me. There's no taste in nothing. I mean to have something of my own. Perhaps it's in Mozambique, perhaps not. But I'm not going to find it if I don't look.'

He belched and swallowed the last of his brandy. He was much drunker now. The brandy on top of the gin was beginning to tell. He tossed his glass into my lap and got to his feet. For a moment he swayed, then he walked stiffly away and went below.

The following morning I signed on as second assistant *commissaire* and gave Captain Van Bunnen one hundred and twenty-five of my two hundred dollars.

I hated parting with the money but at that moment it seemed the only thing to do. I thought I was buying a few days of time in which I wouldn't have to think.

2.

I was ashore for less than three hours in Port Said—just long enough to get a visa for Mozambique from the Portuguese consulate and to buy the few things I needed. Goutard went off on his own when we left the consulate —to look for a brothel, I suspected—but I returned to the ship. I wasn't taking any unnecessary chances. It was a relief to be back on board again.

Early next morning the *Wolvertem* joined the south-

bound convoy through the canal for Suez. We didn't
stop long there and I didn't go ashore. Soon we were on
our way again, down the Gulf of Suez toward the Red
Sea.

"*The arsehole of the world*"—that's what my father
used to call the Red Sea. He had been through it in a
troop ship in summer, and two soldiers—men who had
been in India and were used to heat and humidity—had
died of heat stroke. He had told me that, even on the big
P. & O. liners, the Red Sea in summer could be very dangerous for elderly passengers and people with heart disease. Nowadays, of course, liners on that route are air-
conditioned.

The *Wolvertem*, however, was neither a liner nor air-
conditioned; moreover, she had a defective ventilation
system.

I suppose I should have been thankful that it was late
September and not July or August, but even so it was
absolute hell. A suffocating wind blew, the sun poured
down and the iron deck fittings became too hot to touch.
On the third day out from Suez one of the officers told
us that the sea-water temperature was twenty-eight Cen-
tigrade, well over eighty Fahrenheit. The nights were almost as bad as the days. It was impossible to stay in the
cabin. We slept on deck. Even know-it-all Goutard had
to admit that it was worse than anything he'd encountered before, even in North Africa.

And then the condenser trouble began again.

I don't know anything about ships' engines. Goutard
said that the trouble had to do with sea water leaking

from the condenser cooling pipes into the fresh water of
the boilers. If such leaks weren't stopped, it appeared,
they could soon disable the ship completely.

The faulty condenser in the *Wolvertem* had only been
patched up in the repair yard at the Piraeus. Now it
would have to be patched up again. It was hoped, though
not very confidently, that the other condenser would
hold out until we reached Aden.

By the fourth day out from Suez we were limping
along at reduced speed; and, naturally, the slower we
went the hotter it became. In the engine room the temperature rose to a hundred and forty. It didn't feel like
much less in the dining saloon.

That afternoon we got the news by radio that there
was a dockyard strike in Aden and that we would have
to put into Djibouti in French Somaliland for repairs.

That evening I made a perfectly ghastly mistake.

It was Captain Van Bunnen's fault entirely. The trouble with the ship, the radio messages to and from the
owners' agents in Aden, the prospect of having to dock
for repairs in a strange port—all that *plus* the heat had
been too much for him. He passed out two hours earlier
than usual.

As a result, Goutard joined me on the deck long before it was time to sleep; and he brought with him the
best part of a bottle of the Captain's Dutch gin. He sent
me for the tooth glasses. Then we began to drink the gin
and talk. I'd had a few drinks earlier, of course, and, because of the heat, very little to eat. I became—well, not
exactly plastered, but far too relaxed.

We talked about the voyage for a while. Goutard didn't mind at all that we were going to have to put into Djibouti. In fact he seemed to be looking forward to it. He thought he might find some old army pals there. From that he got onto some of his army experiences in Indo-China and Algeria.

There is always something infectious about that sort of talk. Get two old soldiers together and, if one starts remembering, it won't be long before the other starts too. Then the stories can go on for ages, the truth and the lies all mixed up together, with nobody much caring which is which as long as the lies make some sort of sense and the truth isn't too incredible.

Of course, I am not, strictly speaking, an old soldier, but because of my father I sometimes feel like one. That is natural enough, I think, but you have to be careful of feelings like that; they can be a trap. If you feel you are something and aren't very careful, you may forget yourself and really believe for a while that you are what you feel. It doesn't always matter, but sometimes it can matter a lot. You can land yourself in a Godawful mess.

It all started with a comment I made.

He had been talking about the different ways in which men behave in battle. Then he told me about an officer he had served under who had been a stickler for the regulations and a paragon of efficiency and decision until he actually came under fire for the first time, when he became totally helpless. As it was Goutard telling the story, it had naturally been Sergeant Goutard who had been forced to step in, take charge and save the day. The officer had later transferred to a lines-of-communication unit.

"I know the type," I said; "all piss and wind." That was an expression of my father's. He used it frequently when referring to senior officers. Translated into French, it sounded rather weird.

Goutard laughed and asked me to repeat the phrase. I explained its origin.

"Your father was a British officer?" he asked curiously.

"Oh yes. I was one of the barrack rats."

I had to explain "barrack rats" to him then—that it was a British Army slang term for the children of regular serving soldiers brought up in barracks and cantonments.

I ought to have stopped there, but he was looking really interested. "Soldiering's in my blood," I said. And then, for good measure, I repeated another of my father's axioms, "*If a man parades with a clean rifle you don't need to ask him if he's wiped his arse.*"

This was more difficult to explain, but I got the idea over in the end—first things first. Of course, Goutard didn't realize that I was still quoting my father; he assumed that I was now expressing my own ideas.

"Where have you served?" he asked.

The question should have warned me, but I was feeling reckless by then.

"Libya, the Western Desert."

"Eighth Army?"

"As far as Tripoli."

It wasn't completely untrue. I *had* served with the

Eighth Army, in fact, as civilian interpreter for the Army Catering Corps purchasing office in Cairo. If helping to stop those bloody Egyptian black-marketeers selling food poison to the GHQ officers' mess wasn't serving with the Eighth Army, then words have no meaning. On two occasions I was personally thanked by the warrant officer in charge. But none of this was really in my mind as I talked to Goutard. I just wasn't thinking. I was being somebody else.

"What rank?" he asked.

"Lieutenant,"

"What arm?"

"Intelligence. I speak Arabic."

"Ah yes. Of course."

"Though I never fired a shot in anger."

"No?"

"No. I was just one of the targets."

He grinned. "Wounded?"

"Not a scratch." I was grinning too now. "Unless you count a broken ankle."

"How did you get that?"

"On a long-range desert group patrol. Some Luftwaffe boys found us and tried to shoot us up. I decided I'd prefer to be under my jeep rather than in it while the fun and games were on. I just jumped out a bit too quickly."

Understatement is the rule for this kind of conversation. You have to signal early that you're not out to make the other man feel that he can't top your story with one of his own.

Goutard chuckled, as I had expected he would. Actu-

ally I had overheard a Northumberland Fusiliers corpo-
ral tell the story in the NAAFI canteen at Heliopolis in
1941.

After that Goutard did most of the talking. All he
wanted from me was the occasional right word to show
that I thoroughly understood what a tough guy he really
was. That wasn't difficult. I may not have had much personal experience of war but I do know something about
soldiers and soldiering. I can sense when a man is bullshit-
ting. Goutard wasn't. In fact some of the things he told
me about—what he'd done to some Algerian prisoners,
for instance—would have made me a bit sick if I hadn't
had a few drinks inside me. As it was I laughed. And I
laughed, of course, because I was afraid not to do so. I've
already admitted that he scared me from the start.
There's no use pretending otherwise. That's why what
I did was such a stupid mistake.

What I did was make him believe that I was telling the
truth about myself.

With a man like Goutard you can't make a stupider
mistake than that.

What clinched it, I think, was a single ill-advised remark I made.

He had been going on about the Indo-China campaign
and about some ex-Nazi Germans he'd known and liked
who were in the Foreign Legion at the time of Dien Bien
Phu.

"Good soldiers," he said, "real professionals, if you
know what I mean." Then he glanced sideways at me.
"But you were never a professional, were you?"

"No, but I know what you mean."

He swung around to face me. "Do you? Well, then, what *do* I mean?"

I hadn't expected to be taken up suddenly like that. For a moment I didn't know what to reply. Then I remembered another saying of my father's, one that had always rather puzzled me. I thought it might puzzle Goutard.

"*The important thing is to get there*," I said, "not *die like a bloody hero in the attempt.*"

For a moment or two he went on staring at me; then he smiled and nodded.

"Yes," he said, "that is one kind of professional approach."

He leaned forward and emptied the rest of the gin into my glass.

3.

Two days later we crawled into Djibouti.

There was a strong offshore breeze and the *Wolver-tem* had to be warped alongside the mole, where she was to remain until the repair yard was ready to receive her.

French immigration and customs officials came on board to attend to the formalities and we were given transit visas to cover our stay there. It was understood that for the moment we would eat and sleep on board the ship. We could not continue to do so, however. It was estimated that the repairs would take at least a week, and, when work began, the drainage pumps and other machinery on board would be shut down. During that time we would have to live ashore.

That was all right for the official crew, whose pay would continue and whose living expenses would be borne by the ship's owners. It was not all right for Goutard and me.

We had a difficult half hour with Captain Van Bunnen.

He had taken our money on the understanding that he would transport us to Lourenço Marques and provide room and board on the way. But he had done so unofficially. Our "signing on" had been a paper formality for the benefit of the Port Said, Suez and other port authorities. The ship's owners were unaware of our existence and would doubtless remain unaware of it. We were thus personal guests of the Captain and so, logically, should have continued to be his guests while we lived ashore.

At least that was what *we* said. The Captain, however, was disinclined to view the situation logically. He held that the delay was in the nature of an act of God for which he was in no way responsible. And if he was not responsible for the delay, he could not be held responsible for any inconvenience it caused.

Goutard handled him rather well that time. Obviously we were in no position to get tough. He was the legal captain of a ship and technically we were members of his crew. If we appealed to the local authorities and revealed the truth, he might have to answer some awkward questions, but then so would we. If he chose to say that we had boarded the ship illegally and without his knowledge and suggested a cable inquiry to the police in Athens, we could very well spend our days in Djibouti in jail.

On the other hand it was very much in his interest that there should be no trouble with the civil authorities. The owners already had troubles enough with the *Wolvertem*. A captain who added to them would be decidedly unpopular.

Having tactfully pointed this out, Goutard proposed a compromise solution. We would pay for our meals ashore if the ship would pay our hotel expenses. They could be entered in the books, Goutard suggested, as additional bribes to repair-yard officials.

After some haggling the Captain agreed, subject to our notifying him in advance of the cost per day of the hotel accommodation. In the afternoon we went ashore to make inquiries. A taxi took us into town.

It had been raining heavily and there was a strong smell of hot mud. This was scarcely surprising; there was mud everywhere. The whole place seemed to be one vast mud flat with roads across it built on causeways. There were a few small bushes along the sides of the roads but the mud itself was barren. There were no trees. On the outskirts of the town there were clusters of ramshackle native shanties built out of oil drums and bits of packing cases. The people living in them were mostly Somalis, very tall and dignified with shiny black faces and brightly colored turbans. Some of them wore striped djibbah-like robes. In the town itself, though, most of the people were wearing European clothes—white trousers and short-sleeved shirts. I saw Indian and Arab names on some of the shop signs.

Because Djibouti is both tropical and French I had expected it to be in some way picturesque. It isn't. It is just a lot of square stone buildings and bare treeless streets. They say that the only tree that does well in Djibouti is a palm that was specially imported. This tree doesn't die because it was never alive; it is made entirely of zinc. The thought of spending a week there was depressing.

There is an important railway terminal at Djibouti—it is the railhead for Ethiopia—and, consequently, several small hotels. The one we chose was the Hotel de l'Europe. The proprietor was an Armenian and he was willing to reserve a room for us and make a special price for the week; most of his guests were transients. It was a run-down place and the water that came out of the taps was brackish, but the drains seemed to be working and the Armenian possessed a DDT spray as well as a fly whisk. It smelled reasonably clean.

That was Monday. We moved in on the Wednesday.

On Saturday I met Fate in the person of Jean-Baptiste Kinck.

4.

Between the hotel entrance and the Armenian's office there was a small courtyard partly roofed over to make a place where guests could sit in comparatively cool air and be served drinks. I had been sitting there the previous evening when Kinck had arrived.

Goutard had been invited to a club by some ex-Army friend whom he had run to earth in the Commissariat of Police, so I was alone. I noticed Kinck partly because I was so bored that any sort of happening, even an arrival or a departure, was of interest, and partly because his general appearance struck me as unusual.

He was in his early forties, I judged, tall and wiry with a narrow head and short gray-brown hair. He was wearing khaki drill slacks and a bush shirt with a large sweat stain on the back of it. Over his right shoulder was slung a leather and canvas haversack. His complexion was pale but he moved in a way which suggested drive and nervous energy. My first impression was that he was some sort of minor government official from the interior. Then the Arab boy who swept the courtyard and acted as porter came out for the newcomer's luggage and I had to revise my ideas. The luggage consisted of an expensive-looking lightweight suitcase, a portable typewriter and a much-used Sabena airline flight bag. An oil technician? I wondered. Or a newspaperman? He could have been either; but in that case, why the Hotel de l'Europe, why not one of the bigger hotels?

I gave no more thought to him then; but the following evening, on returning to the hotel after getting a haircut, I found him in the courtyard deep in conversation with Goutard. They had beers in front of them.

I hesitated to join them; Goutard's reactions to my company were not always predictable. Then Goutard caught sight of me and waved me over.

Kinck stood up to shake hands when Goutard introduced us. He had better manners than Goutard but the same considering eyes. They were brown and narrowed slightly when they looked at you, as if he were short-sighted or you were reflecting too much light. He had a tight, sweet smile and very good teeth—rather a handsome man in an angular sort of way.

Goutard said expansively: "Monsieur Kinck has been telling me about things I have never even heard of before. They are called 'rare earths.' "

"They sound interesting."

"Interesting and expensive. Do *you* know what they are?"

"Something you mine out of ordinary earth, I imagine."

The Arab boy came up and I ordered a beer. I was thinking that my guess that Kinck might be some sort of mining engineer hadn't been a bad one.

Kinck smiled. "If you can get at them to mine, you mine them, yes. But generally it is not so simple. Have you ever heard of ilmenite?"

"No."

"Or rutile?"

"No."

"They are ores of the metal titanium."

"I've heard of that," Goutard put in quickly.

"Of course you have. It is being used now in the making of supersonic aircraft. It is in fact a very common element, and much more abundant in the earth's crust than, say, lead or tin. Yet the current world market price of titanium is in the region of three thousand dollars per metric ton."

"Three thousand *dollars?*"

"Certainly. And why? Because titanium, though common, is difficult to mine. There are other metals still more difficult. Have you ever heard of pyrochlore?"

Obviously we hadn't. I was beginning to lose interest in Kinck, but Goutard was all attention. For once he was willing and eager to be told something.

"Another rare earth?"

"Technically an ore, but certainly rare and precious. It contains the metal niobium now much in demand for high-temperature alloys and nuclear sheathing. The current world price of niobium is plus or minus one hundred and ten thousand dollars per ton."

Goutard whistled.

Kinck shrugged. "Mining used to be simple. Some mining is still simple. You dig out the ore, you crush it, then you discard the part you don't want, by washing it away perhaps, and you smelt what is left. It is as simple almost as cracking a nutshell to get at the nut." He clenched his right hand into a fist to demonstrate nutcracking.

"But not with niobium," Goutard prompted.

"Not as a rule, no. Pyrochlore is found usually only in small quantities and as a small percentage of very large quantities of other ores. It must be concentrated by complex *dressage* processes involving magnetic and mechanical separation, flotation, leaching-out and chemical separation. You may have to process many tons of other material to obtain only a few kilos of pyrochlore." He turned to me. "So, you see, it is expensive. There are other such materials which are still more expensive."

I had to say something. "Is that your job," I asked, "prospecting for this sort of stuff?"

Goutard chuckled. Kinck smiled. Apparently there was some private joke between them that my question had blundered into.

Kinck's eyes slid back to me. "Well, not exactly, Monsieur Simpson. The people I work for still prefer nutcracker methods." He got another chuckle from Goutard. "But you might say that I am a prospector," he went on. "Yes, I think you might say that."

Goutard really laughed that time. Kinck smirked complacently into his beer glass. I made myself smile. I hate other people's private jokes and being treated like a half-wit, but I've learned that it's better not to show it.

When Goutard had had his laugh, Kinck looked at me again. "My apologies, Monsieur. What I was explaining to our friend Goutard before you joined us was that there are many other valuable substances in the world besides gold and precious gems and uranium. Can you imagine what a concentrated, high-yield deposit of one of these special minerals is worth? Almost as much as a diamond field, *and*—" he leaned forward slightly—"it is almost as difficult to secure and protect. For that purpose one needs men of experience and resource. Of course, such men are not easy to find, but—" he leaned back and smiled again—"where there are great rewards to be had there are always difficulties to be overcome. That is in the nature of things." He glanced at his watch and then got to his feet. "It has been a great pleasure talking to you. I shall be here for a few days. I hope that we will meet again."

He shook hands with us briskly and left, calling for the boy to get him a taxi.

Goutard was grinning and lighting a cigarette.

"What was all that about?" I asked.

"Didn't you guess? I thought he made it plain enough. He's recruiting."

"Men of experience and resource?"

"That's one way of putting it." He was looking thoughtful now. "My pal in the Commissariat knows about him. There is quite a dossier on our Major Kinck. Nothing criminal, but interesting."

"*Major* Kinck?"

"He wouldn't use his military title here. But I'll bet he's using it somewhere. He flew in yesterday from Lamy in Chad. That doesn't mean that he's based there, of course, but it's an indication of his present working area." He let smoke drift from his mouth and inhaled it up his nose—one of several unpleasant habits he had—then looked at me with his rat-trap grin. "If we weren't going to Mozambique," he said, "I might be tempted to ask him how much he's paying."

5.

Captain Van Bunnen was not living in a hotel but in the private bungalow of one of the Messageries Maritimes officials. As this was in the European residential quarter, we had not seen anything of him since the ship had been towed into the repair yard and he had given Goutard our hotel expenses for the week. We kept in touch with the situation through young Bergier, the Third Officer, who used the same restaurant as we did when he wasn't on anchor watch in the ship.

The *Wolvertem* had been in the yard five days when he broke the news to us that he had been told officially that she would be there five more days. His unofficial opinion was that she would be there for at least fifteen, and at that we would be lucky. He was going by what the Chief Engineer had told him about the extent of the repairs needed and the shortage of the skilled labor required to do the job quickly. He had also heard that there had been talk of transshipping the cargo, the owners of which had now lost patience, and of sending the *Wolvertem*, when she could be made seaworthy, in ballast to Mombasa.

"Is that a serious possibility?" Goutard asked.

Bergier shrugged. "With the *Wolvertem* nothing is serious and anything is possible. We have loaded cargo in Mombasa before—coffee, tea, sisal, chemicals. Perhaps we will again, if we ever have the strength to steam there."

"Where would such a cargo go?"

"To a European port, naturally. But this is all rumor and gossip, you understand. I *know* nothing."

He knew enough to ruin my appetite.

Later, Goutard and I talked over the situation.

Even if we discounted the rumor about Mombasa, the outlook was bleak. We were having to buy our own food, and money was already short. I had managed to sell the Greek drachma I had had on me for Djibouti francs so as to conserve the dollars, but those francs had already gone. Another ten days ashore would see the dollars gone too; and I had to reckon with the real possibility of an even longer delay with no money at all to live on.

Goutard wasn't much better off than I was. As a Frenchman stranded in a French overseas territory, he could probably have obtained repatriation at government expense, but he didn't seem to like that idea. From the way he rejected it I gathered that his return to metropolitan France would have been about as sensible at that time as a return to Greece, and woud have had disagreeable consequences of a similar nature.

The obvious answer, according to Goutard, was to re-negotiate our agreement with Captain Van Bunnen. Goutard said that we would have to be firm. "Discreetly menacing" was the phrase he used. Those were his actual words.

The following morning we went out to the laurel-hedged bungalow where the Captain was staying and caught him as he was about to leave for the ship. He had his usual hangover, of course, and was anything but pleased to see us. There was a taxi waiting for him. If Goutard hadn't planted himself squarely in front of him as he reached for the taxi door I don't think Van Bunnen would have stopped for us.

Unfortunately he did stop.

"What do you want?" he demanded irritably.

"Just to talk, Captain. A matter of business." This was Goutard, of course. He had taken charge. I was just there. I was in no way responsible for what happened.

"It will have to wait," Van Bunnen snapped. "I am in a hurry now. I must go out to the ship."

He reached again for the door handle. Goutard got his hand on it first.

"All right, Captain," he said, "we'll go with you."

Van Bunnen hesitated. Goutard was holding the door open, but although his attitude was polite his face had a very unpleasant look on it. Van Bunnen took a second look at him and then climbed into the taxi without a word. We climbed in after him.

It was a small Renault and we were all crammed together. I was already sweating with the heat. Inside the taxi the sweat began to run down into my eyes. Only Goutard remained cool. As we drove off he eased around on the seat to face Van Bunnen, who tried unsuccessfully to look impassive.

"Well," he said curtly, "state your business."

"Money," said Goutard. "We are going to need more money."

"I gave you hotel expenses for a week. That was the arrangement."

"But now we are going to be stuck here for more than a week."

"That is a matter outside my control."

"No doubt. But *we* are still *inside* your control, Captain. You have a responsibility. We ask simply that you discharge it."

"We made an arrangement to which you agreed."

"Circumstances have changed. So the arrangement must change. It *will* change, Captain."

"That is for me to decide."

"Yes. As long as your decision is realistic."

Goutard went on to outline the facts. I must say he did that part of it very well. He was calm and reasonable. He made it clear that we were not trying to make money, but simply to avoid being unjustly penalized by the delay. He asked what would happen if he, a Frenchman, had to go to the authorities—he mentioned his friend in the Commissariat—and apply for assistance on the grounds that he was destitute. Naturally, he would have to explain why he was destitute. Inquiries would be made, questions asked. Finally, he appealed to the Captain's well-known good nature and reminded him of the friendly evenings they had spent together. I could see that Van Bunnen was weakening.

Then we drove into the dockyard and all of a sudden everything became insane.

It was a remark of Van Bunnen's that triggered the explosion. In itself the remark was innocent enough, but it made insufficient allowance for the possibility of Goutard's patience, already overstrained by his effort to be persuasive, suddenly becoming exhausted.

What Van Bunnen said as the taxi stopped by the ship was "Well, I will think about it." He then opened the taxi door and started to get out.

That was it.

Goutard made a sort of angry gargling noise in his throat and jabbed a foot out.

It caught Van Bunnen in the behind and sent him sprawling forward onto the concrete pier.

There was a Somali dock policeman standing there, and at first, I think, he believed that Van Bunnen had merely tripped. He started forward to help him up.

But Goutard was already out of the taxi and reached Van Bunnen first. As the Captain scrambled to his feet, Goutard grabbed him by the shirt and began to shout in his face and shake him.

"So you'll think about it, will you, you drunken sack of shit? Well, think now and think fast, Captain Sinbad, because I'm on your back and not letting go. You understand? You think *now! Now!*"

Van Bunnen, recovering from his surprise, began to yell back and attempted to hit Goutard. The latter swept the blow aside and jabbed the heel of his hand hard into Van Bunnen's face.

"*Now,* Captain Sinbad! *Now!*"

The policeman stared uncertainly at the struggling white men and hefted the long truncheon he carried, but all he *did* was to start shouting too. The Indian driver and I were out of the taxi by now and everyone was shouting. Then there was a sound of running footsteps. The next moment young Bergier and the Chief Engineer had an apoplectic Goutard by the arms.

Van Bunnen backed away quickly. There was blood trickling from his nose. As he dabbed at it with his handkerchief I saw him look from us to the policeman. I was sure that he was going to have us arrested. Then he seemed to think better of it. There was a chance that we could still make trouble for him. He decided to forestall that by disposing of us formally.

"These two men are dismissed from the ship," he said loudly.

Goutard yelled an obscene reply.

"For insubordination," added Captain Van Bunnen. "They are lucky that I do not charge them with striking a superior officer. I may yet do so if they give any more trouble."

He turned and walked up the gangway to the ship. Goutard wrenched his arms free and started after him, but the policeman was ready to act now. He moved quickly to the foot of the gangway and barred the way.

Goutard turned furiously on Bergier.

"That sack of shit took a hundred and twenty-five dollars from each of us."

"I know," said Bergier, "but there's nothing I can do

about it. He's the skipper."

I had what I thought was a very ingenious idea.

"We were signed on as crew," I said. "Is it legal for the Captain to dismiss us in a foreign port of call, no matter what the reason, without paying us off?"

Bergier looked at the Chief Engineer. "What do you think, Chief?"

The Chief thought for a moment, then grinned. "Perhaps not. Perhaps we will ask him."

They went on board. Goutard and I waited. Then the Indian driver was at our elbows wanting to know who was going to pay the taxi fare. I thought Goutard was going to go berserk again. I promised hurriedly that the fare would be paid as soon as the officer returned.

Twenty minutes later Bergier reappeared. He was smiling and he had some papers in his hand.

Two of the papers were receipts for us to sign. The rest of the paper was money—the equivalent in Djibouti francs of fifty dollars U.S. apiece.

Goutard burst out laughing, clapped me on the back and gave me a crushing handshake. You'd have thought he'd just inherited a fortune.

When we had signed the receipts and Bergier had handed over the money, he got a handshake, too, and an invitation to celebrate over dinner. Even the driver was included in this outpouring of good will. Goutard announced that he could drive us back to town.

I was learning fast that the more I saw of Goutard the less I understood him. I hadn't thought him capable of such wild changes of mood. Now, in the space of forty minutes he had swung from sweet reason to violence, and then from violence to a sort of idiot euphoria. The euphoria was thoroughly disconcerting. He couldn't seem to realize what had happened. In the taxi on the way back I tried to point out that, while we had begun the day as delayed but still hopeful passengers to Lourenço Marques, we were now only fifty dollars away from being stranded on the beach at Djibouti. All I got was another hearty slap on the back. I gave up. Being slapped on the back by Goutard was like being hit with a flatiron.

He had to come back to earth that evening, however.

Bergier brought the bad news when he turned up for dinner.

It appeared that Van Bunnen, having brooded over the indignities he had suffered that morning, had decided that if we could be legalistic about being paid off, he could be legalistic about his duties as a ship's captain. As a result he had formally advised the police that we had been paid off and dismissed from the ship for refusing to obey orders.

Goutard's first reaction was to shrug and then order a bottle of wine. I took Bergier's warning more seriously.

"What will it mean to us?" I asked him.

"Well, it means that the police here will take an interest in you now."

"Why?" demanded Goutard. "We have done nothing."

"That is not the point. You must understand that seamen in a foreign port are generally in a privileged position where the police are concerned. If they do not get helplessly drunk or start fights or smuggle too openly, they are left to come and go as they please. And why? Because tomorrow or the day after or next week they will be gone. They belong more to the ship than to the shore. But in your cases things are now different. You no longer belong to the ship, and the police have been told that you don't."

"I don't see anything different about it." Goutard was being willfully obtuse.

Bergier sighed. "The reason you were allowed to land here without question is because you were a member of a ship's crew in transit. That reason no longer exists."

"Have some wine."

Bergier's tone sharpened. Goutard was beginning to irritate him. "Will you be able to show merchant seaman's papers when the police come asking for them?" he inquired. "If not, do you have a visa for the territory?"

Goutard smiled cryptically and got to his feet. "If it will put your mind at ease," he said, "I will telephone and find out if the police are interested."

He went off to telephone. Bergier stared at me.

"He has a friend in the Commissariat," I said.

Goutard was gone some time. When he returned he explained that he had had to contact his friend at a club.

"And?" I inquired.

"We have nothing to worry about."

He said it too casually. I guessed that he was lying. It was a stupid statement anyway; we had plenty to worry about apart from the attitude of the police. However,

Bergier seemed to accept it.

"It is always useful to have friends in high places," he said dryly.

No more was said on the subject until we had said good night to Bergier and were walking back to the hotel.

"What did your friend really say?" I asked.

"We have three days."

"Then what?"

"Then they will want to know what we propose to do and what means of support we have at our disposal. If our answers are unsatisfactory we shall get our marching orders. He advises, though, that we do not wait to be called in and questioned but apply immediately for a permit to remain one week. That would probably be granted. But it would not be renewed."

There was no need to comment on that; one week would see the end of our money anyway. In a week we would be down-and-outs.

I said nothing to him for a while. I was tasting the bitterness. Thanks to Goutard's irresponsibility we had been chucked out of Greece. Thanks to Goutard's irresponsibility—his physical attack on Captain Van Bunnen had been senseless—we were going to be chucked out of Djibouti.

But chucked where? Onto a rubbish heap? Into jail? I was trying to think of a last hope to hold onto but couldn't. The far end of the creek—the muddy, murky, closed end—was in sight.

"What are you going to do?" I asked.

I asked because at that moment it seemed to me that anything that Goutard did must inevitably turn out badly. If I could in some way do the opposite thing it was possible that my luck might change.

He glanced at me and grinned. He was quite sure of himself again. "There's only one thing left *to* do," he said.

"What's that?"

"Talk to Major Kinck."

6.

Their talk took place the following afternoon. I was not present.

It had been a most unpleasant day. We had decided to take Goutard's friend's advice that we should forestall the police inquiries by presenting ourselves at the passport control bureau and applying for permits to stay for a week. The move had not proved as disarming as we had been led to expect. We had been questioned and cross-questioned anyway. The police couldn't have been worse. The questioner was a suspicious and bloody-minded Frenchman who made it clear from the start that he regarded us as undesirables. Goutard had the worst time—because he, too, was French, I suppose—but I didn't do much better. My passport was received with a mocking smile. The bastard wouldn't take our word for anything. We had to show our money and count it out before his eyes. Then the amounts were written in our passports. We were warned against attempting to find work, unless it was in a ship leaving Djibouti, or to engage in the drug traffic. We were told, finally, that if either of us was still in the territory seven days hence, he had better be able to swim. Even Goutard was subdued when we left.

He was going to meet his police friend for lunch and I was glad he was. During the night I had made some sort of a plan and I didn't want to discuss it with him.

Aden was only one hundred and fifty miles away by sea across the Bab el Mandeb strait. I thought that if I could get to Aden I might be able to land a job as a steward on one of the boats that stopped there. They didn't know me in Aden, and anyway it was a busier port than Djibouti. I had no union card, of course, or seaman's papers, but I thought that some of the cargo-liner captains might not be too particular about that if they happened to be short-handed.

I made inquiries about ferries to Aden and found that there was one that did the trip in nine hours. Or I could get there by air in one hour. The sea route was the cheaper, so I went to the shipping-company office to buy a ticket.

The man had already started to make out the ticket when he stopped and asked to see my passport. I handed it to him and he thumbed through it. Then he looked up.

"Where is it?"

"Where's what?"

"The visa for Aden."

"I'll get it there."

"Ah no. That is not permitted, except for those with British passports. You must obtain the visa here. Otherwise the British will refuse you permission to land and we will be obliged to bring you back. There is much trouble in Aden at present. We do not issue the ticket until the passenger has the visa. That is the regulation."

"Where do I get the visa?" But I had already guessed the answer to that.

"It is issued by the British Consul."

I thought of H. Carter Gavin again and what I would have liked to do to the young swine, but I didn't waste time going to the consulate. My name was in the black book and all I would get there would be insults. Instead, I spent the afternoon at the port. There were trading dhows that made the trip to Aden and the Yemen and I was desperate enough to try anything. Eventually I found one Arab dhow master who was willing to put me ashore near Aden, but he wanted the equivalent of a hundred dollars to do it. That was what he would be fined, he said, if a British patrol boat caught him. He was a smelly, evil-looking bastard and I didn't believe a word of it. Even if I'd had a hundred dollars I'd have thought twice about trusting myself to that man. Most likely he would have taken my money and dropped me over the side as soon as we were out of sight of land. I told him in Arabic what he could do with his dhow. He recognized my accent and called me a filthy Egyptian.

I'd been on my feet all day and was very tired, but I couldn't afford taxis; I walked all the way back to the hotel. I felt half dead by the time I reached it.

In that sort of climate you have to drink plenty of fluids if you want to avoid heat prostration and kidney trouble, so I had two or three bottles of beer before ordering what I really needed to counteract my depression —a double brandy.

As a result I didn't really have all my wits about me when Goutard returned.

"Where have you been?" he demanded as he sat down beside me.

I started to tell him. Since my Aden plan hadn't worked out there was no longer any reason for keeping quiet about it. Besides, I was in a generous, philosophical mood. Arthur Abdel Simpson might be *persona non grata* with the British—and up the creek and on the skids —but if Yves Goutard, French citizen, wanted to go to Aden he could probably get a visa without trouble. Why shouldn't he know it? I may have failings but being a dog in the manger is not one of them.

I was explaining all this to him when, in his worst ill-mannered way, he cut me short.

"Aden!" he said impatiently. "Who the hell wants to go to Aden? Listen! I have talked to Kinck."

"Oh?"

"He has a very interesting proposition."

"Has he?"

Even that minor interruption nettled him. "Do you

want to hear about it or don't you?"

"Of course."

"I told you he is recruiting. I was right. Here is the proposition. A three months' contract, renewable for further three-month periods by mutual agreement. Terms, two thousand Swiss francs a month basic salary —that is nearly twenty-five hundred French francs— plus all traveling and living expenses, plus equipment allowance, plus fifty percent bonus after six months. One month's salary to be paid in advance on signature of initial contract. There! How does that sound?"

It sounded like Paradise to me and I had a sharp twinge of envy. "What's the job?" I asked.

He smiled his most confident and knowing smile. "Just showing some stupid *macaques* how to secure and protect a strip of land."

"One of these deposits of rare earth?"

"Of course. You heard what he told us."

"Where is it?"

"He won't say yet. Naturally, he has to be careful at this stage. But it isn't either of the Congos. I told him right away I wouldn't be interested if it were. He assured me it isn't. Farther north, he says. We leave by plane on Thursday."

The boy brought him a beer. I raised my glass.

"Well, good luck to you."

"Good luck?" He raised his eyebrows. "Is that all I get? No thanks?"

"What for?"

He bristled. "Don't tell me you don't want the job.

Where else can you get that kind of easy money? You knew I was seeing Kinck. If you weren't interested why didn't you say so?"

I gaped at him. "Me?"

"Who else are we talking about?" He was getting angry again. "I went to a lot of trouble to convince him about you and it wasn't until I told him about your record that he agreed to take you."

"My record!" I was appalled; all I could think of was my Interpol record. "Why did you have to do that?"

"Well, nowadays you don't exactly *look* like Eighth Army and Western Desert, *do* you? Naturally, he wanted to know about your soldiering experience. Now you say you're not interested. What's the idea? I don't like being made to look a fool. What sort of a game do you think you're playing?"

His face was beginning to take on the pinched look it had had just before he had hit Captain Van Bunnen. It scared me. I knew that I had to stop him quickly or he would hit me.

"I'm not playing any game. I just didn't realize that I was included."

"I said *we*, didn't I?"

"Yes, but I thought you meant you and—"

"We're together, aren't we?" he broke in accusingly. "Why should you think we weren't? I'm not one to rat on a pal."

"No, and I'm very grateful. Have a brandy."

"I was going to." Suddenly his grin was back in place. He was really quite unpredictable. "No more worrying about the sous, and we won't have to learn to swim after all." He chuckled. "A good feeling, Arthur, eh?"

"Very good."

And it *was* a good feeling while we went on drinking.

It would have been still better if it had not been accompanied by an anxiety and a suspicion.

The anxiety was immediate enough. The frying pan out of which I was jumping I knew all too well, and bloody uncomfortable it was; but what was the fire going to be like?

The suspicion, on the other hand, grew slowly. I had already noticed that Goutard was a man who had to have someone to fetch and carry for him. Perhaps, I thought now, the need went beyond that. "We're together, aren't we?" he had said. He had also, in a moment of rage, called Van Bunnen "Captain Sinbad." Even at the time I had thought that rather peculiar. It could be that he was the kind of man who had to have a Sinbad in his life. If so, it was more than possible that, without realizing it, I had already been cast for the role.

The prospect of having Goutard as my Old Man of the Sea was one I didn't care to contemplate.

7.

At eleven the following morning we reported to Major Kinck in a room at the offices of a trading company near the railway terminal. There were three other "recruits" besides Goutard and me.

Kinck was seated behind a table beside a wizened man with a neat stack of papers in front of him. Extra chairs were found and he asked us all to sit down.

He began by introducing the wizened man beside him. "This is Monsieur Pauwels, business and purchasing agent for the Société Minière et Métallurgique de l'Afrique Centrale, which is to be your employer. It is understood and your contracts will stipulate that you are employed by SMMAC purely and simply as security officers." He paused and then added blandly, "You are in no sense members of a military or paramilitary organization. Is that correct, Monsieur Pauwels?"

The wizened man nodded gravely. "Quite correct. SMMAC does not employ private armies."

Kinck smiled. "Indeed not. That would be most illegal."

There was a murmur of amusement. He went on in a more conversational tone.

"You gentlemen of experience are becoming hard to

find. I had *hoped* to find eight or more of you here in
Djibouti. However, as I only *expected* to find four and
have found five, I am not too disappointed. Other
sources have provided an advance party. Our total
strength in the area of operations should now be sufficient. But let us get to business. I shall start by identify-
ing each of you to the others." He picked up a typewritten
list. "When I read out your names please raise your
hands."

He began to read, giving the surnames first.

"Barrière, René. Formerly lieutenant in the French
Army. Infantry. Active service in Senegal and Upper
Volta. Later military-police duty in Dahomey. Weapons
instructor. Recent experience in customs enforcement
and border-patrol work in this territory. Speaks some
Swahili."

Barrière was in his late thirties, a stocky, cold-eyed
man with blue jowls and dark hair cut *en brosse*. He
nodded to the rest of us as he raised a hand.

"Goutard, Yves," Kinck went on. "Formerly sergeant-
major in French Army. Paratrooper and brigade paratroop instructor. Active service in Indo-China and
Algeria. Recent experience in transport and security
organization. Speaks some Arabic."

Presumably Goutard's "experience in transport and security organization" was another name for his job with
Hayek.

"Ruys, Johannes. Formerly sergeant in Netherlands
Army. Engineer specializing in explosives and demoli-
tion. Active service in Europe and Indonesia. Recent ex-

perience in road and bridge construction, South Africa and Tanzania. Fluent German and English, good Swahili."

Ruys was about my age, I think, a big ox of a man with pale eyes and skin reddened by exposure to the sun. He fidgeted with an unlit pipe and looked as ill at ease as I felt. I wondered why he had left South Africa and Tanzania.

"Simpson, Arthur. Formerly lieutenant in British Army. Field intelligence officer. Active service in Egypt and Libya. Long-range desert patrol work. Recent experience in commercial security organization. Fluent English and Arabic."

I sweated.

"Willens, Adrian. Formerly squadron leader in South Africa air force. Active service in Burma. Long experience as professional hunter and wild-animal collector in Kenya and Ethiopia. Active service in Mau Mau period. Fluent English, Afrikaans and Swahili." Kinck looked up before he added waggishly: "French with a horrible accent."

That got a mild laugh. Kinck, of course, was speaking in French, which was the *lingua franca* of the group.

Willens didn't seem to mind the joke at his expense; he merely shrugged. He was in his late forties, lean, dried up, thin-lipped, his face and neck brown and seamed like a walnut. He looked cool, good-humored and tireless.

Major Kinck put his list down. "You will be meeting your colleagues of the advance party in two or three days. Now, as to pay and allowances, Monsieur Pauwels will explain the procedure."

Monsieur Pauwels rearranged the papers in front of him. He was compulsively tidy.

"As you have been told," he said, "there will be an advance of salary on your signing the contracts which I have here ready. This advance will be paid in francs CFA—" he meant French African Community francs— "which is the currency you will be using generally in your area of operations. However, I should inform you that you are unlikely to need much ready cash there, as your major living expenses will be provided for by SMMAC. I believe also that you will not wish to accumulate large sums in this field by receiving your salaries in cash." He had a very attentive audience now. "There are, therefore, two alternative methods of payment from which you may choose. If you have a current banking account in the European community or sterling areas, SMMAC will pay you by draft direct to your bank. If you prefer a simpler arrangement we can provide you with a paybook and periodically credit you with the salary due to you by entries in the book. The sums due would, of course, be obtainable on presentation of the book at any of SMMAC's offices, including their head office in Geneva, or at the offices of their agents, including this one. If necessary, sums could also be obtained in the field and the amounts debited in the book. However, cash, bank or paybook, it makes no difference to SMMAC. The choice is entirely yours."

He referred to a sheet of notes.

"Next, some married officers may wish to transmit allowances to their wives or other dependents not accompanying them. SMMAC is willing to arrange this. The sums in question would naturally be deducted from those officers' salaries. Are there any questions at that point?"

Goutard asked, "Do we draw uniform allowances?"

Kinck answered, "Uniforms will be supplied to you from SMMAC stores. No payment will be involved."

"How about inoculations?" This was Barrière.

"I was coming to that. Most of you will already be fairly well covered, I imagine. However, it is as well to be prudent. I find that the hospital here has a yellow-fever inoculation period between three and four o'clock tomorrow afternoon. You will also need a certificate of smallpox vaccination. I have arranged that any of you desiring them can have shots for typhus, typhoid and tetanus at the same time. A typhoid booster is recommended if your last is over two years old. You should start taking anti-malaria tablets. Anything else?"

There were no more questions. Monsieur Pauwels took over again. "Then we will proceed to the contracts. They are, you will find, in a very simple form. If you will come to me as your names are called we can get the business done in an orderly manner. I will need to retain your passports so that certain necessary visas can be entered in them before your departure on Thursday."

We went up in the alphabetical order of Kinck's list.

The contract was a two-page document on SMMAC's Geneva head-office letter paper and three copies had to be signed, one of which was given to the recruit. Then the advance of salary was paid over. I was interested to

see that nobody asked for his salary to be paid into a
bank; they all took paybooks. Monsieur Pauwels seemed
to have expected this; there was a paybook already made
out for each of us. The stuff about needing our passports
for visas I took with a grain of salt. It seemed to me that
they were holding our passports as a form of insurance
against any of us deciding to take the salary advance and
forget the contract.

The sight of the money on the table was good, though.
When it came to my turn I did my best to look as if what
Kinck had read out about my army record were true. I
almost succeeded in convincing myself.

I might have maintained that attitude but for one
thing. Right at the end of the contract there was a place
where you had to write in the name and address of your
next of kin.

I wrote in Nicki's name and our address in Athens.
Where you stated the nature of the relationship I put
"sister." I wasn't going to make her a marriage allowance, of course, because she didn't need one, but I didn't
want to look mean.

It was thinking about that that made me hesitate; and
hesitating made me read the whole paragraph.

"*In case of the aforementioned officer's death, wound-
ing or disablement through disease, his next of kin, re-
corded by him below, shall be immediately informed.*"

I signed the contract, I took my copy of it, I took the
paybook, I handed over my passport and I took the
money; but I didn't feel like a soldier any more. I was
feeling sick.

Part Three

Journey to a Rare Earth

One

Early on Thursday morning we assembled again, with our baggage, at the offices of SMMAC's agents and were handed back our passports. I looked through mine immediately. To my surprise I found two new transit visas in it, one for the Sudan and the other for the Republic of Chad.

There was a minibus to take us to the airport. Barrière and Willens had their wives with them and we were all introduced. The two women got into the bus with us. Naturally I assumed that they had come to see their husbands off. The fact that they were both wearing slacks and shirts I saw merely as an attempt on their part to enter into the campaigning spirit of the occasion which I found so depressing. The idea that they might be coming along too never occurred to me. I wish it had. For me it might have made the ride out to the airport seem less like a journey to the dentist. I hadn't slept a wink the night before and had dirty gray moths fluttering in my stomach.

After we had been through customs and passport control we got back into the bus again and were driven around the perimeter to a freight hangar. A scruffy-looking twin-engined plane sat on the tarmac outside. We piled out of the bus and, still carrying our luggage, climbed aboard.

I had realized by then, of course, that the two women were coming along with us, and so was feeling a bit more cheerful. The place we were going to couldn't be too uncivilized, I thought, or they wouldn't be there. That meant that the soldiering part of it, which I had really been dreading more than anything else, would probably turn out to be no more than a kind of garrison duty. In that case I probably knew enough and could guess enough to get by. Kinck had said that we were security officers, not a private army. I wanted to believe him.

The interior of the plane was less reassuring than the train of thought I had been so carefully assembling.

For one thing it had no seats in it. At least it *had* seats, but not the kind you ordinarily expect in a plane; these were just small aluminum stools bolted along both sides of the fuselage and fitted with springs to flip them up out of the way when they weren't in use, or when you stood up for a moment to straighten your back. Most of the space was occupied by a long stack of crates and metal boxes lashed down with wire cables to cleats on the battered metal floor. The plane had been standing in the sun and the heat inside made even Kinck recoil.

"It'll be cool enough once we're in the air," he said. "Just dump the bags anywhere and get your seat belts on."

We squatted on the stools—the curve of the fuselage made it impossible to sit quite upright—and the sweat dripped from our noses and chins. Willens was next to me with his wife next to him. I heard him say something to her in English: "Vintage World War C-47 with the original bucket seats," he muttered. "I hope these bird-men know what they're doing."

Then one of the crew, a pale man in khaki shorts, shut the door and the engines were started. After that all normal conversation ceased. The plane wasn't sound-proofed; nor was it pressurized. I don't know how high a plane of that type can fly, but it wasn't high enough for me. There were times when we were flying with the mountaintops above us. Fortunately it wasn't possible to see much; the air was so bumpy that we had to keep our seat belts fastened, which made it difficult to look out of the windows without dislocating your neck. As Kinck had promised, it became quite cold.

After an hour or two the air was smoother. Lunch cartons containing fruit, cheese and stale bread were passed around, together with bottles of wine and water. Nobody ate much, but the wine went quickly. Personally I needed it; and not only because the flight scared me.

Sitting crouched on that hard seat with my elbows on my knees, all I had to look at was that section of the cargo immediately facing me. There was lettering visible on some of the boxes, though on those I could see best it was upside down. After a while I began idly to make out the words and figures.

The first word I made out was UZI with a dash and the figure 4 after it. That word could have told me a great deal, but it didn't; I thought then that it represented initials. On the next crate to it the letters could only be initials because they were punctuated. They read F.N.—M.A.G.–7.62. A heavy pressed-metal box interested me most. There were several others like it. The one nearest to me had the word MORT stenciled on the top. That alone would have been fairly discouraging, but the positioning of the letters made it clear that MORT wasn't the whole word. By bending down and pretending to loosen my shoes I got a look at the rest. The whole word was MORTIER and it had some figures after it and some more letters that I didn't attempt to decipher. MORTIER and the figures were enough. Now all I had to do was to wonder why an advance party of security officers, on their way to take up commercial appointments somewhere in Equatorial Africa, had to be accompanied by eighty-two-millimeter mortars.

My watch had stopped, but as the hours went by Willens began to look at his frequently. He seemed to like what he saw less and less. Finally, he pulled out paper and pencil, made some calculations and took the results over to Kinck. They had a bellowed mouth-to-ear conversation from which I gathered that if we didn't land soon we would be out of fuel. Kinck went forward to consult the crew and came back smiling and making signs with his hands to indicate that we would be landing in approximately ten minutes.

Willens returned to his seat but kept his eyes glued to his watch. Then the plane tilted slightly and my ears began to hurt as we lost height.

The place where we landed that day was Juba, a town on the White Nile in South Sudan. The passengers spent the night in the airport rest house. The crew stayed with the plane—to guard the freight, presumably.

That evening Kinck's authority was challenged for the first time.

Willens was evidently still brooding over the length of the flight. The almost uneatable dinner may have made him a bit edgy too. We were all still at the table drinking coffee when the argument started.

Willens pushed his coffee away with an exclamation of disgust and then looked across at Kinck.

"Are we permitted to know tomorrow's flight plan?" he asked. His tone was vaguely belligerent.

Kinck smiled. "Certainly. From here we fly to Fort Archambault in Chad."

"Refueling where?"

"Refueling nowhere. We fly direct."

"Do you know the maximum range of a C-47 at normal cruising speed?"

"The pilot does."

"Well, so do I. It's not much more than two thousand kilometers."

"Archambault is not that far."

"Perhaps not, and thank God we won't have to do quite so much mountain-dodging as we did this morning, but what about headwinds? What happens if there's a navigational error? That's not the newest equipment you have there."

"The crew are highly experienced."

"I'm not saying they aren't. But over this sort of country and in these latitudes the best of navigators can make mistakes. They ought to be allowed for. We ought to give ourselves time to correct them."

Mrs. Willens chipped in. She was Australian and in her thirties, a tall, sexy-looking brunette with amused, no-nonsense eyes and a wide mouth. "My husband flew four hundred hours piloting C-47s," she said. "He knows what he's talking about." Her French accent was better than his.

Kinck smiled at her courteously. "I am sure he does, Madame. I'm sure we all know what we're talking about. I certainly do."

"If we refueled at Yalinga we'd be taking no chances," Willens persisted.

"We are taking no chances by flying direct."

Willens appealed to Goutard. "What do you say, Goutard? You know something about planes."

"Only about jumping out of them." He winked.

Madame Barrière laughed. She was a chunky little woman with an urchin face. Her laugh was very loud. It broke the tension somewhat. Kinck took advantage of the fact.

"Anyone who is nervous can have a parachute," he remarked casually.

Willens and his wife didn't join in the laughter. I did, though my sympathies were really with Willens. He stuck to his point.

"Personally I'd prefer a forced landing in the bush," he said. He looked at Kinck again. "What's wrong with a refueling stop?" he demanded.

"Only that it is unnecessary."

"In your opinion."

"Yes." Kinck's face tightened up. "But mine is the opinion that counts. I may add that if a refueling stop in Yalinga or anywhere else were advisable, we would not be traveling to our destination via Archambault."

"What *is* our destination?" Barrière wanted to know. "Why all the mystery? We'll have to know sooner or later."

"I prefer that you know later. When you *need* to know." He looked around a trifle coldly at the rest of us. "It should not be necessary to explain the need for prudence to security officers, and I must remind you that in a disciplined force, movement orders are not subject to discussion." He stood up. "We will be making an early start in the morning. I suggest that you all get plenty of sleep. Good night."

He bowed slightly to the two women and left.

There was a brief silence, then Barrière made a disrespectful plopping noise with his tongue.

There were a few snickers but nobody made any other comment. Ruys produced a flask of whisky and passed it around. When we had had a drink we went off to bed.

I was sharing a room with Goutard.

"Well," he said as we were undressing, "what do you think?"

"I don't quite know what to think. Willens seems to know what he's talking about and he doesn't sound like an alarmist. After all we did run things a bit fine today."

"But we got here, and with fuel to spare. Don't forget, I saw Kinck's dossier. He doesn't strike me as a man who would take unnecessary risks."

I felt like saying that I didn't want to take risks of *any* kind, not even the necessary ones, but that wouldn't have been soldierly. Instead I said the second thing that came into my head.

"Perhaps he's just being cagey."

"What do you mean?"

I didn't know what I meant, so I had to think fast. I made a big production of taking my trousers off so as to give myself time. "Well," I said finally, "he talked about the *need* to know, and he said he'd prefer us to know where we were going later rather than sooner."

"What about it?"

"One asks 'why?' Where's the security risk? We're traveling as a group. Who could we talk to except ourselves?"

"But the walls have ears. We could be overheard talking. Is that what you mean?"

"Not exactly." I tried to sound as if I were continuing a single line of reasoning but a different one had suddenly intruded. "We're carrying arms in that plane," I said.

"Of course we are. I'm not blind. Light automatic rifles and machine pistols—hand weapons. What about it?"

"We're carrying mortars as well," I pointed out. "They're not hand weapons. You can be sure that the security people here as well as customs have inspected them. They will be very interested in their destination."

"So?"

"That means that they will be interested in *our* destination too. We're an armed party. Supposing they decided to interrogate us separately. They might very well do that. What would happen? If we all knew what our ultimate destination really was and had to lie about it, they'd soon catch on. Even if we all tried to tell the same lie one of us would be bound to give the game away. Lying under interrogation isn't as easy as people think. As it is, though, we don't have to lie. All we know is that we're going to Archambault in Chad and we have visas in our passports to show that we intend to. We have nothing yet to lie about."

Goutard was sitting on his bed now, naked, hairy and grinning; he had no modesty at all.

"Once an intelligence officer always an intelligence officer, eh, Arthur?" He was pleased with me.

I shrugged and turned away. "It's obvious when you come to think of it."

"Yes." He slid under his mosquito net. "No wonder Kinck's not interested in refueling stops."

"How do you mean?"

"If what you say is correct, I should have thought that also was obvious. Refueling won't be necessary because we're not really going to Chad, but somewhere nearer. Perhaps we won't even be going in the same direction. Once we're clear of this area we can change course and go anywhere we like."

"Anywhere Kinck and SMMAC like, you mean."

"It's the same thing, isn't it?"

"I suppose so."

But I didn't really think that it was at all the same
thing.

It wasn't.

2.

As I had predicted, the Sudanese airport officials gave
us a real going-over before they cleared us for Chad. We
even had to turn out our pockets. They were polite, but
in a very snotty way—trained by the British, of course.

And, as Goutard had predicted, we did not go to
Chad. Twenty minutes after we were airborne Kinck
sent around a message he had scribbled on SMMAC
paper.

It said:

"*Please note and pass on. Change of flight plan has
been made. Detour to Archambault no longer necessary.
Therefore now proceeding direct to destination. Ap-
proximate flying time 4½ hrs. Further briefing later.*"

I passed it on to Willens. He glanced at it, then gave
me a wry look. Obviously he was feeling now that he'd
made an ass of himself the night before. I smiled at him
sympathetically. After all, he'd thought he was acting in
all our interests, and I'd liked the way he stood up for his
opinion. He wasn't used to dealing with tricky bastards
like Kinck, I thought.

We were given the briefing instead of lunch.

It turned out to be three mimeographed sheets, a copy for each of us, which Kinck produced from some hiding place in the crew's quarters. It described our destination in some detail.

At this point I may as well make one thing plain. While I am prepared to be completely frank and open about *what* happened, I am not prepared to compromise myself by showing that I know exactly *where* it happened. Our destination is clearly marked on any reasonably up-to-date school atlas, and the authorities there—and other interested parties—may do all the guessing they want, but I'm not making any admissions that might be used in evidence against me by unscrupulous persons in official positions. I have changed the place names not "to protect the innocent" or any nonsense of that sort, but to protect *me*.

This was, more or less, how the "briefing" read:

SOCIÉTÉ MINIÈRE ET MÉTALLURGIQUE DE L'AFRIQUE CENTRALE
Kawaida Regional Office: Kundi, Republic of Mahindi

CONFIDENTIAL

Information for the guidance of
SMMAC personnel proceeding to
Kundi Province, Republic of Mahindi

POLITICAL HISTORY

The Republic of Mahindi was one of the colonies of French Equatorial Africa offered independence by France in 1958. In the subsequent referendum Mahindi

*voted for autonomous association within the French
Community. In 1960 she exercised her option to become
completely independent. Her relations with France, however, and with most members of the French Community
in Africa continue to be cordial. She is a member of the
U.N. A boundary dispute with the neighboring Republic of Ugazi is in process of being submitted to the International Court at The Hague.*

*Legislative powers in Mahindi are exercised by a forty-
five-member Assembly elected for a five-year term. For
administrative purposes the country is divided into five
provinces each sending nine members. The Assembly sits
in the capital city of Mkubwa (pop. estimated 1965:
185,000) for two periods of three months annually. The
President, who is elected by the Assembly, is currently
Monsieur Paul Nyoroka. This is his second term of office.
His administration has been termed "a one-party democ-
racy."*

*This is not to say, however, that he is all-powerful.
The authority of the Central Government outside the
capital is exercised through the provincial governors and
is by no means uniformly effective. It is weakest perhaps
in Kundi Province, where, for reasons which will become apparent, there is a considerable measure of local
autonomy.*

There was more political guff of this sort. Then followed some geographical guff with descriptions of the
land and the climate.

In Mahindi, it appeared, they had everything from

jungle and rain forest to swamps and bush and desert; and there wasn't anywhere which didn't get either too much rain or too little. Everywhere and at all times it was hot, though, so you were either in a steam bath or a roasting oven no matter where you went. In short, if the Red Sea was the arsehole of the world, the Republic of Mahindi was its left armpit.

The people didn't sound any more reassuring than the place.

In the country as a whole the predominant ethnic group is Bantu with some Mbaka and Banda in the south-central provinces and Fulani Berbers in the north, mainly in Kundi.

It is the concentration of this substantial Fulani Berber minority in Kundi which gives that province its special character. It should be understood, however, particularly by those with North African experience, that the word "Berber" is here used solely in an historical ethnic context. Although the Fulani of Kundi are Muslims, speak Arabic and regard themselves as racially superior to the Bantu, their color and appearance are more Negroid than Caucasian or Hamitic. The Hausa of northern Nigeria come from the same stock and now have the decisive political voice in Nigerian affairs. The Fulani of Kundi have a political voice in the affairs of Mahindi which, if not yet decisive, is certainly stronger than that of any of the other racial minorities in the Republic.

They went on then to talk about Kundi Province itself. It was in the northwest corner of Mahindi and was

about the size of Belgium. There was more double-talk
about climate and rain, from which I gathered that it was
half steam bath and half oven. Its western boundary was
the Nyoka River, which was also the frontier between
Mahindi and the next-door Republic of Ugazi.

They slipped in that last bit about the Nyoka River
very casually, the bastards.

Then they became all highfalutin.

*The Governor of Kundi Province is His Excellency
the Emir Othman dan Fuado. He is also, by right of descent, spiritual leader and ruler of the Fulani community
in Mahindi.*

*The Emir is in some respects a controversial figure. He
has been denounced by opponents in Central Government circles as a feudal autocrat and despot with designs
on the parliamentary system (such as it is) and the Re-
publican Constitution of 1959. In Kundi, where he has no
opponents (or, at least, none who raise their voices), he is
seen as practicing a necessarily firm, but on the whole
benevolent, paternalism. He is known to refer to himself
on occasion as the* Baraka *(blessing) of Kundi.*

*In forming any general opinion about the Emir's ad-
ministration it is necessary to be strictly pragmatic.
Against his regrettably overdeveloped taste for public
executions and the somewhat Gestapo-like organization
of his palace guard must be set the fact that, in this essentially primitive society, order is maintained and property
rights respected. This cannot be said of some other provinces in Mahindi.*

SMMAC'S relations with the Emir and the officials ap-

*pointed by him are extremely cordial. It is intended that
they shall remain so. No criticism of the Emir's administration or officials on the part of SMMAC personnel will
be tolerated. Offenders will be instantly dismissed.*

*A further word of caution. The Fulani of Kundi are
proud, intelligent people. The men have a strong sense of
personal dignity and are highly sensitive to ridicule. An
ill-timed joke can be more offensive than a blow. It is
recommended that European personnel practice the utmost discretion at all times.*

*The position of Fulani women in Kundi (many of
whom are very handsome) is somewhat unorthodox for
a community professing the Muslim faith. It must be remembered, however, that the Fulani are* au fond *a mixed
race. That they should adopt and practice at least some
characteristic Central African customs is scarcely surprising. One custom in particular should be mentioned. This
permits the head of an important village family to present
an unmarried man whom he wishes to please with one of
his daughters for use as a concubine. Unmarried European personnel should be prepared to deal tactfully with
this situation. The woman offered in these cases is invari-
ably nubile and delivers herself to the recipient's house
without ceremony. Nevertheless, polite refusal of such
gifts may in the long run be wiser than their acceptance,
as, once accepted, they are extremely difficult to return.
(See also notes on* HEALTH.)

On that happy note they got back to business again.
The province had two marketable crops, cocoa in the
south, cotton in the north. Around the villages near the

three major towns vegetables were grown for local consumption and some sheep and cattle grazed. The vegetables mentioned were sorghum, taro, manioc and beets. It didn't look as if I were going to be tempted to put on weight.

The information still flowed thick and fast.

The major towns in Kundi are FORT GREBANIER (*pop. estimated 1965: 65,000*), *which is also the Provincial Capital;* MATENDO, *a river port on the Nyoka; and* KAWAIDA, *which is the center of our tungsten and cassiterite operations. A light railway managed by SMMAC personnel connects Kawaida with our Matendo facility, where processed ore shipments are transferred to barges.*

I noticed that they still hadn't said anything about the rare-earth area we were supposed to guard. This stuff that they were shipping out by light railway and barges didn't sound very rare. I plowed on through the rest of the briefing.

There are fair roads between these towns, that between Fort Grebanier and Matendo being asphalted for much of its 180 kilometers. There is a small airport outside Fort Grebanier and a SMMAC air strip at Kawaida. Such telephone and telegraph facilities as exist are unreliable. SMMAC employs short-wave radio for most local operational purposes and routes cables through Ugazi, where the telegraph service is still supervised by European personnel.

The briefing concluded with a merry little piece on the subject of health.

HEALTH

For mentally well-adjusted persons, free from high blood pressure and adverse heart conditions, the Province need not be unhealthy. Good health in Kundi, as elsewhere, is largely a matter of common sense, self-discipline, correct diet and attention to personal hygiene.

Among the diseases to be met with in Kundi Province are bilharziasis, leprosy, ancylostomiasis (hookworm), filariasis, ascariasis (worm infection), yaws, dysentery of various kinds and venereal diseases. Epidemics of typhus, yellow fever, relapsing fever, smallpox and meningitis may also be experienced. Endemic are trypanosomiasis (sleeping sickness) and malaria, though attempts by government teams working under World Health Organization advisers to control malaria have met with some success in the populated areas in and adjacent to the towns. Deficiency diseases are common among the natives, but as these are largely due to ignorance of dietetic needs they do not concern us here.

The following rules should be observed at all times:

NEVER *drink or brush the teeth with water that has not been boiled or chemically purified. The addition of alcohol to water does not purify it.*

NEVER *swim or wade in unchlorinated water.*

NEVER *eat food that has not been thoroughly cooked.*

NEVER *eat fresh fruit or salads.*

NEVER *drink fresh milk that has not been boiled, or powdered milk prepared with unpurified water.*

NEVER *eat cooked food bought from street vendors.*

NEVER *neglect to wash the hands* thoroughly *before eating or after any contact, direct or indirect, with excreta, including your own. It must be assumed that any man-used object touched in the course of the day's work is a likely source of infection. Always endeavor, when possible, to avoid inhaling dust.*

NEVER *neglect to take malaria precautions.*

NEVER *permit yourself to become depressed. A positive, cheerful attitude is mandatory. Good health is as much a matter of morale as of prophylaxis. Physical exercise promotes morale. At our Kawaida club facility, tennis courts are available for the use of European personnel.*

ALWAYS *remember that good health is a duty you owe to yourself and your family, not simply an obligation to your employer.*

WELCOME TO KUNDI

They might have added AND LOTS OF LUCK, JACK, but maybe they didn't want to start you off feeling *too* positive and cheerful.

3.

We landed at Fort Grebanier in the early afternoon.

There was a huge bank of black cloud shaped like a toadstool hanging over the airport and, as we began taxiing in, it let go. Sheets of rain came down, swamping the runway and reducing visibility to about three feet. We sat there in the plane and sweltered until the downpour eased off a little and visibility improved. After a while a truck with a canvas top and SMMAC lettering on its sides backed up to the plane door.

Kinck had said that this was only a short stop for Mahindi passport control and that there would be no customs examination. We left our bags in the plane and were ferried in the truck to the terminal building, a verandahed shed with a corrugated iron roof and big unglazed window spaces to allow the air to circulate. As the air was uniformly hot and humid and smelled of rotting wood, mildew and stale urine, it really didn't matter whether it circulated or not.

Inside, Kinck had a brief private conversation with the local SMMAC representative who was there to meet us, and then we were led to a desk behind which sat a severe-looking black man. He wore a white short-sleeved shirt, a dark tie and a striped Muslim cap. Beside him stood a turbaned policeman, equally black, with a long leather-covered truncheon swinging from a strap looped to his wrist. The policeman looked us over with angry, blood-shot eyes and swung his truncheon as if he were hoping for an excuse to use it.

The SMMAC man ignored the policeman and spoke to the passport man in a language I only just recognized as Arabic. It was very curiously accented.

He said: "These are the persons about whom business visa arrangements have been made with the Commissaire."

The man at the desk looked even more severe. "I understand," he replied; "but there will be fifty francs stamp duty to pay for each of the visas as well as twenty-five francs a head entry tax."

His expression suggested that he expected his statement to be disputed. When the SMMAC man merely nodded and started counting out the money the man behind the desk stared at it sullenly. Obviously, since there had been no bargaining, he now realized that he might successfully have asked for more. I was quite interested. There were eight of us in the party. One franc CFA is worth a fiftieth of a French franc, so all he was making for himself out of the whole transaction was the equivalent roughly of two U.S. dollars, or twenty-five cents a head. It's not everywhere that you can get past a passport control official with a twenty-five-cent bribe. And with a policeman looking on, too! The Republic of Mahindi, I thought, might have possibilities after all.

By the time he had gone through the motions with his

three rubber stamps, his violet ink pad and his ball-point pen, I was feeling almost cheerful.

The truck took us back to the plane, which presently floundered through the mud and slush into the air again. Our destination this time was the SMMAC airstrip at Kawaida, and that, temporarily, would be the end of our journey, according to Kinck. He had emphasized the "temporarily" but still hadn't said anything about our ultimate destination. Not that I cared much about that; all I wanted was to get back to earth safely.

We ran through a lot of cloud on the way to Kawaida and were thrown about violently once or twice, but over Kawaida itself the sky was more or less clear. As we began the descent I craned around and had a look through the window.

At first the country below looked like a lot of dark-green moss without distinguishable features. Then as we got lower I could see that what I was looking at were tree-covered hills. Suddenly the green was broken by a series of long red gashes which converged on a sprawl of big shed-like buildings connected by dirt tracks. There was earth-moving machinery working there and a contraption that looked like a giant hose. A long fat jet of dirty water spouted from it into the red hillside. Then we were racing over some smaller, symmetrically arranged buildings which could have been houses or army huts. Ten seconds later we were bouncing along the airstrip.

It had been bulldozed out of the jungle, and the thin coating of asphalt which had been put down was already seamed and potholed. We jolted to a standstill finally in front of a makeshift hangar, a lean-to affair made of tubular scaffolding with a corrugated iron roof but no walls. A light plane sat beneath it and some stacked fuel drums. A SMMAC truck stood waiting.

This time the cargo received first priority. We had to climb down the rickety steps and stand about while the cases were off-loaded by the plane crew and the two men with the truck.

The latter were both white and obviously this was not their normal work; they were almost clumsy in the way they handled some of the heavier crates. But, just as obviously, they had known in advance what the cargo was and were not surprised to find themselves handling mortars, machine guns and boxes of ammunition. Kinck supervised and now and again lent them a hand, but there was no conversation. Their silence was infectious. Nobody in our group said anything either; we just stood in front of the hangar and tried to fight off the swarms of flying insects that soon attached themselves to us.

The sun had begun to go down by the time the truck was loaded. Darkness came while we were climbing into it. Kinck had a flashlight and kept it on while we found seats on the crates and boxes. The crew were maneuvering the plane into the hangar. A Volkswagen arrived to pick them up as we left.

We drove off the strip in low gear and then up a winding track. The truck sides were slatted and in the reflected glare of the headlights we could see thickets of trees with long, tattered leaves bordering the track. Willens said that they were wild plantains. The smell of corruption, of things rotting beneath fungus growths, was very strong. The insects came along with us.

After a while the track ended in something more like a road, and for a minute or two we were on level ground. Then we slowed and the driver sounded his horn and flashed his lights. After some vague shouting we picked up speed again and drove through an open gate in a high chain-link fence with lights overhead.

When we were through the gate two black men in shorts with slung rifles started shutting the gate behind us.

"The SMMAC compound," Kinck said; "we generate our own electricity."

Now we were among the small buildings I had seen from the air—rows of whitewashed cinder-block bungalows on concrete foundations built clear of the ground.

"These are the houses of our European personnel," Kinck went on. "Some, as you see, have air-conditioners. For this part of the country they represent the ultimate in luxury. But, of course, those who live in them are on long-term contracts."

"Is this our base?" Barrière wanted to know.

"No, this is merely our assembly point. But we will talk business later. You must be hungry. I must apologize for the breakdown in the arrangements for lunch on the plane. Juba airport was uncooperative. Perhaps we can make up for that soon at the club."

I wasn't particularly hungry, but I was tired and thirsty. Willens echoed my own thoughts.

"Does the club have a bar?" he asked.

"Oh yes. And the locally brewed sorghum beer is quite safe."

The truck had turned a corner and stopped outside a bungalow similar in construction to the others but twice the size.

"This is the SMMAC guest house for transient personnel," Kinck explained. "At the moment we have a chemist and a geologist visiting the facility, so there are only three rooms available. Some of you will be a little crowded, I realize, but it will not be for long. The house boy has his orders and will show you where to go. He won't steal from you, by the way. Your possessions are quite safe while you are inside the compound. The club you can see from here." He pointed to a cluster of lights about three hundred meters away. "I suggest that we meet at the bar in an hour."

Inevitably, the married couples appropriated two of the available rooms. Goutard, Ruys and I were crammed into the third. The showers were in a separate concrete washhouse behind the bungalow, but there were four of them and plenty of water in the roof cistern. By the time I had cleaned up and changed my shirt the others were ready, too, and we all went together. As I walked down the guest-house steps something scuttered across the path in front of me. I stopped. Willens was just behind me.

"Only a rat," he said and Mrs. Willens chuckled.

I walked on, but from then on I looked very carefully where I was going. Just the idea of rats terrifies me. How a sexy-looking woman like Barbara Willens could laugh at them I don't know.

The club was built of the same materials as the bungalows and was in a compound of its own along with the
advertised tennis courts. Someone had tried to cheer the
place up by plastering Air France and Sabena travel post-
ers on the bare walls, but the only effect of that was to
make it look like a travel bureau. The unglazed window
openings were screened to keep out the insects, but they
came in through the doorways anyway. Ceiling fans re-
volved without cooling. In the bar there were lounging
chairs fitted with long extension arms so that the men
could dangle their legs over them and air their crotches.
One or two were doing so. The few wives there were in
sloppy cotton frocks and so had a different solution to
that problem. There was a bridge four in one corner and
two men at the bar itself were playing poker dice. There
was little conversation. The predominant sound was that
of a diesel generator thumping away steadily somewhere
in the compound. But everybody looked up when Kinck
rose to greet us. Most of the personnel at Kawaida were
in their thirties; all of them, both men and women, had
the same pasty, yellowish look about their faces which I
had noticed in the men who had met us with the truck.
The only suntan visible was on some of the arms and
hands.

In spite of the stares, Kinck didn't introduce us to anyone; he merely nodded, smiled and led the way into a
room beyond where there were more chairs and a ping-
pong table. A boy came. Kinck ordered eight beers and,
when the boy had gone, leaned forward confidentially.

"Perhaps I should explain now," he said, "that, as SMMAC European personnel, you are automatically entitled to use the facilities of the club. Special identity cards will be issued to you tomorrow in case you are questioned. That is unlikely, of course, because every European here is a SMMAC employee, but unfamiliar faces naturally excite curiosity and when chits are signed by newcomers names have to be checked. I would, however, recommend that in view of your rather special and confidential security role, you avoid making friends or acquaintances with other employees. As I said, you will not be here for long. Your own operational area will be some distance from here, and the less that it is discussed at present, except among yourselves, the better."

Barrière shrugged. "Since we don't yet know anything about it, we can't even discuss it among ourselves."

Kinck smiled amiably. "That situation can be remedied when we are less thirsty and hungry, and when there are fewer ears to hear what is said." He glanced up significantly at the boy who had arrived with the beer.

It didn't taste like beer, but it was cold and wet and surprisingly strong. I was feeling better when we went to dinner, which we had in the cafeteria used by the unmarried European employees. The food was quite eatable— all out of cans, but I don't mind canned food—and there was more beer, as well as boiled water served in old screw-top brandy bottles. Wine, Kinck explained regretfully, was not available in Kawaida. The cost of importing it was high, it spoiled rapidly on arrival and, in the opinion of SMMAC medical advisers, it was an unsuit-

able and potentially harmful drink in that climate. The
French pulled long faces over this news, naturally, and I
pretended to do so, but I didn't really care. With beer
and brandy available, I thought, I could face the future
and perhaps survive.

After dinner Kinck suggested that, as Madame Barrière and Mrs. Willens were doubtless tired from the
journey, they would probably wish to return straight to
the guest house. In that case he would ask the men to pay
a short visit to his office to discuss their plan of work.

The two women took the hint.

Kinck's office was in the administration compound, a
group of four standard bungalows behind yet another
wire fence. Among the painted metal signs on the door
of the fourth bungalow was one which read SECURITÉ—
MAJOR KINCK.

Kinck unlocked his office door and switched on an
air-conditioner as well as the lights.

"We will need two more chairs," he said over his
shoulder. "Bring them from the next room."

No more "pleases." Monsieur Kinck was now Major
Kinck again.

Ruys and I fetched the extra chairs and sat down with
the others. One wall of the office had sheets of plywood
fastened to it. On the plywood were pinned plans, aerial
photographs and several maps of the kind which are
made by surveyors and reproduced in blue ink.

Kinck sat on his desk and looked down at us.

"Well, gentlemen," he said, "welcome to Kawaida."
Then he gave us his sweetest smile. "I am afraid that the

time has come when I have to tell you that from this moment on every one of you must consider himself as, so
to speak, under arrest."

4.

He was joking, of course, but nobody there seemed to
find it very funny; in fact Ruys looked a bit ill for a moment. Personally I found it a joke in poor taste.

But Kinck went on flogging it to death. "*Open* arrest,
of course," he said, still smiling, "and without, let us
hope, a court-martial in prospect, but still with certain
inconveniences involved."

Still nobody smiled. He gave it up and became businesslike.

"As security-minded persons," he continued, "you
will realize that where important and valuable secrets are
concerned there can be no such thing as trust. So, as it
now becomes necessary for me to share some secrets with
you, I must first ask you to accept some temporary restrictions on your personal freedom. Is that understood?"

We nodded.

"It will be simplest then if from now on you consider
yourselves as commissioned officers on active service in a
theater of war and obliged to observe a code of strict

security regulations. Specifically, you will, from now on, write no letters nor correspond in any other way with outside persons without submitting such letters or messages to me for censorship. You will not communicate verbally with civilian personnel here or in the operational areas to which you will be going except in the presence of a brother officer or unless you have specific orders to do so. These restrictions apply also to wives. I may add that for a period of two months from now none of you will be permitted to leave Kundi Province for any reason or on any pretext. Is that all understood?"

"What about illness?" asked Willens. "Supposing my wife gets sick. Anyone could in this sort of place."

"We have adequate medical facilities here at Kawaida with a fully qualified European doctor in charge. Any other objections?"

Willens shook his head, rather reluctantly, I thought.

"Then we are all in agreement? Barrière?"

He asked each of us in turn. When we had all said "yes" he nodded.

"Very well, then we can get to work." He reached down, opened a drawer in his desk and pulled out a sketch pad and pencil. "I take it that you have all read carefully the briefing sheets you were given this morning?"

We all nodded.

"Good." He was like a bloody schoolmaster. "I must now tell you that the briefing contains one misstatement of fact. It says there that the western boundary of Kundi Province, the frontier separating us from the Republic of

Ugazi, is the Nyoka River. That is only partly true. The word 'Nyoka' means 'snake' and if you look at the map you will see why the river is called that. Between Ugazi and Kundi it makes two very sharp turns, like this."

He drew a large S on the sketch pad and held it up for us to see.

"Now," he went on, "you know something of the history of these two countries. They were once French colonial possessions. Kundi Province and Changa Province, which now belongs to our neighbors across the river, were once under the same administration, and, for some bureaucratic reason which need not concern us here, a line of longitudinal demarcation rather than the river line was used as the provincial boundary. When Mahindi and Ugazi became independent states that arbitrary provincial boundary automatically became an international frontier. As a result the present frontier crosses the Nyoka River at three places, like this."

He drew a line straight down through the S and smiled faintly as he showed us the result. "Rather like a dollar sign, isn't it?"

He took his pencil again and shaded the two small D-shaped areas at top left and bottom right of the dollar sign. The top one he marked "Zone A," the bottom one "Zone B." He held it up for our inspection again.

"This could be a very expensive dollar sign for Kundi Province," he said; "and I will now tell you why."

He propped the sketch pad up in front of us.

"Soon after their independence the governments of Mahindi and Ugazi discussed the possibility of making

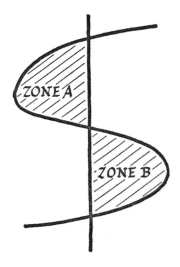

frontier adjustments. These early discussions were quite
friendly. Both sides had already found the old colonial
line inconvenient and absurd. Commercial users of the
river had complained about the delays caused to traffic
by the pointless frontier crossing and recrossing. There
was duplication of effort and expense in several areas—
dredging, for example, and maintenance of customs
posts. Some of these problems were partially solved by
agreement. Traffic clearance procedures were simplified
and other understandings were reached. But it was generally accepted that, sooner or later, there would be
agreement to adopt the river line, the natural frontier, as
the political frontier. The territorial losses and gains
would, as you can see, be roughly equal for both sides,

and there would be gains in stability for both. The riparian and jurisdictional rights of sovereign states separated by so-called 'boundary rivers' are well defined and established in international law. So negotiations continued." He smirked. "Not very rapidly, of course. In this part of the world, where it can take two hours to negotiate the purchase of a bush chicken, negotiations never proceed rapidly. But they continued, and in apparent good faith, until three months ago. Then the Ugazi government's attitude suddenly changed."

He paused to light a cigarette, then blew smoke at us and stretched his mouth wide as if he had tasted something unpleasant. After a moment he went on again.

"Ugazi itself is not, so far as is known, particularly rich in mineral resources. They have some iron ore, though that is not as yet easily accessible, and they are said to have a little manganese. However, a year ago an American–West German consortium signed a mineral exploration agreement with the Ugazi government. Under this agreement the consortium, which calls itself the Ugazi Mining and Development Corporation, received the right to explore for and, if found, exploit all nonferrous metallic ores as well as non-metallic mineral products, excluding oil. This gave them the manganese, if there is enough to make it worth their while, and whatever else they could find. The agreement was made on a royalty basis, and, as soon as the Ugazi Assembly confirmed acceptance of it, UMAD moved in three exploration teams. Five months ago one of those teams crossed the Nyoka at the town of Amari, here—" he indicated the sketch pad again and pointed to the top of the dollar sign where the stroke intersected the S—"and moved south into this country on the Kundi side of the river which I have called Zone A. One month later," he added deliberately, "the Ugazi government announced that it was dissatisfied with Mahindi's attitude toward their river frontier rectification proposals and was therefore breaking off negotiations."

He looked around at us as if inviting comment. Somebody grunted and that appeared to satisfy him.

"Obviously the true explanation had to be different. The Emir, who has his heart set on bringing his people in Zone A, and the land itself, back into Kundi where they belong, asked for SMMAC's confidential advice. As a result we sent an exploration team of our own—secretly, I need hardly say—into Zone A, and ultimately we found what the UMAD team had found. With it we found the explanation of the Ugazi government's sudden strange behavior. On our side of the river, in what is, by every moral, ethnic and geographical standard you care to apply, Kundi territory, there is a deposit of a rare earth with an estimated value of well over a hundred million dollars."

He leaned forward, dangling the sketch pad with the dollar sign under our noses. "SMMAC owns the mineral concessions in Kundi," he said quietly. "I think you will see, gentlemen, why it is necessary that we erase that stroke from the S, and do so quickly and permanently."

He slapped the sketch pad down, got up from the desk and walked around to sit behind it.

"What do we use to erase it with?" asked Willens.

"I will come to that." Kinck seemed irritated by the interruption. "But first the strategic position. The Mahindi government and the Emir have acted and are acting in accordance with our advice. Our advice has been that under no circumstances should the Ugazis be given cause to suspect that we know the real reason for their change of attitude toward the frontier rectification proposals. We do not want them putting troops into Zone A or reinforcing the police they have there already. So far they have done neither. Obviously they do not want to draw attention to Zone A any more than we do at the moment. Second, we advised the government here to take steps to establish its legal claim to the area by formal action at the United Nations and by requesting a hearing of the case by the International Court. They have also offered to submit the dispute to international arbitration. So far this show of good faith has met with no response from Ugazi, whose present policy seems to be to pretend not to hear. Thirdly we recommended that forces from Kundi provided by the Emir should prepare discreetly to move into Zone A and occupy it in sufficient strength to hold it against any attempts at counterattack from across the river. That, gentlemen, is where you come in."

It was where I would have liked to leave. I blurted out the question before I could stop myself.

"As *security* guards, do you mean?"

He gave me a droll glance. "Before an area can be guarded, obviously it has to be secured."

If he had expected a laugh he didn't get it. Suddenly

everybody was asking questions.

"How big is Zone A?"

"What sort of terrain is it?"

"Are there any roads?"

"What forces are maintained there?"

"Are the Emir's men trained soldiers?"

"What happens to Zone B?"

He held up a protesting hand. "All in good time, gentlemen. Everything has been carefully thought out. But I will deal with the question about Zone B first. As I said, we intend to occupy Zone A, which is on our side of the river. However, *simultaneously* we shall withdraw completely from Zone B, which is on the Ugazi side. The population of Zone B is Bantu, not Fulani. Their land and villages are of no value or interest to us. Once we have withdrawn the Mahindi police, border guards and customs officials from Zone B, the whole operation will have simply put into effect the territorial exchange originally proposed and in principle accepted. Our international legal position will be further strengthened by this move, which would clearly be very difficult to reverse."

He waited until he was sure he had us in hand again before continuing.

"Now for your other questions. Maps of Zone A have been prepared and will be available when they are needed. For security reasons we are not issuing them until that time. The sight of one of them could give rise to gossip and that could be dangerous, even within this compound. You gentlemen will be particularly discreet I know because you will realize that indiscretion could

make your task difficult and even dangerous. You need
no security regulations to tell you that."

He let that one sink in.

"Very well. All you need to know at the moment
about Zone A is that it is bounded on the west by approximately eighty kilometers of river line and on the east by
the colonial frontier running between the river town of
Amari in the north and the frontier post near Matendo
in the south. That distance is fifty-five kilometers." He
pointed to the sketch map. "The shape is almost exactly
as I have drawn it here—semicircular. What sort of
country is it? Flat near the river, hilly and difficult elsewhere. Near Amari there are a number of small cocoa
plantations. Amari itself is a sizable town and the Ugazis
have made an administrative center of it. There are villages strung out along the principal road, which in most
places follows the curve of the river. Lesser roads con-
nect the frontier patrol posts outside Matendo, both ours
and the Ugazis'. These were set up in an effort to dis-
courage smuggling by Indian merchants of certain manufactured goods—bicycle parts, for example—which are
dutiable in Mahindi. The interior of Zone A is largely
uninhabited."

"Where is this rare-earth deposit?" asked Willens.

"That we do not need to go into," Kinck replied
firmly. "In fact, it will be better if no further references
are made to that subject for the time being. By securing
Zone A we secure everything in it. No more need be said.
Let us concentrate at present on the military aspects of
our task. I mentioned the Emir's forces. These consist as

far as we are concerned of an infantry battalion armed
with old Mannlicher-Berthier rifles. The battalion has
until recently been deployed by companies and platoons
on what were essentially gendarmerie duties. It is now in
process of being concentrated in a staging area within
striking distance of Zone A. These troops are only part-
trained. They know how to load and fire their rifles,
though standards of marksmanship are not high. They
can use their bayonets. Firmly disciplined under the lead-
ership of experienced European officers, they make good
fighting men. Your colleagues already in the staging area
have instituted a tactical training program which is showing promising results, but they will be glad of your help.
The Emir's own officers are chosen for their noble birth
rather than their intelligence." He paused, frowning, as if
he had momentarily mislaid the thread of his argument.

"Enemy forces?" prompted Barrière.

"Ah yes." Kinck nodded approvingly. "The appreci-
ation in classic form. There is not much to be said about
the opposition. The strength of the Ugazi garrison in
Zone A is estimated at two companies, concentrated
mainly in the Amari area. Most of these men, however,
are normally employed on police duties and at least half
of them are armed only with police clubs."

"How well are they likely to fight?" Goutard asked.

"That depends on who their officers are. I have heard
reports of recent changes. I am expecting more information on that point this week. However, if our own moves
are swift, precise and properly coordinated, there is
every likelihood that they will be too surprised to fight at

all. That is what we hope. The less bloodshed there is the better. We have to consider international opinion. Ideally, the *coup* should end, on the day it begins, with the surrender and disarming of the Ugazi garrison and its repatriation under a flag of truce to Ugazi territory across the river."

"While we get ready for the counter-*coup*," Barrière remarked.

"If it comes. The river is two kilometers wide at Amari."

"But they don't have to counterattack at Amari, Major. They have eighty kilometers of river to choose from. True, we will be on interior lines, but eighty kilometers is a lot of front to hold with one battalion of half-trained infantry. What about transport? How mobile will we be?"

"There will be trucks available for at least two companies to start with, plus a reconnaissance force. Other transport will be commandeered. Don't forget that we expect to have a friendly local population to deal with."

"There should be river patrols," said Ruys. "Boats with heavy machine guns to intercept attempted crossings."

"That too has been allowed for in the plan. The expectation is that, after the evacuation of Zone B is completed, launches and ferryboats will become available for arming as you suggest. However, no final decision on that has yet been made. We have to consider the possibility of reprisals against our river traffic south of Matendo. Our defense against counterattack must remain flexible."

It was almost a relief to hear that the arrangements for
this charming little smash-and-grab raid were not absolutely cut and dried. Somehow that made it seem less out-
rageous. Heaven knows I'm not squeamish, and I've done
a few things in my time which weren't exactly according
to Hoyle, but listening to Kinck talk—well, frankly I
was shocked. What I mean is this. Except for all that
crap about moral rights, good faith and international law
Major Kinck sounded like a travel agent selling a guided
tour to a bunch of half-wits off a cruise liner; he spoke as
if the war he was planning to start was some kind of rib-
bon-cutting ceremony for a much-needed rural development project. My "brother officers" seemed to see it that
way, too. They were listening intently, eyes gleaming,
lapping it up; they really wanted to go ahead; they were
actually *looking forward* to it. They weren't thinking
that they might get killed or injured; they weren't wondering how the hell to get out of it. I was; but then
I think I was the only sane one there.

I heard my name and looked up.

He was asking each of us in turn if we had any further
questions and had come to me.

"Only the obvious question, Major," I said. "When is
D-day?"

"I thought I had answered that," he replied irritably.
"As I explained to Barrière, we expect the Emir's forces
to be up to strength within two weeks. The date for the
operation will be decided then. Ruys?"

"I do not know this eighty-two-millimeter mortar.
What is its effective range?"

I didn't hear the reply. Other thoughts were going through my mind.

5.

It was Ruys, of all people, who put those other thoughts into words.

We were back in our room at the guest house.

Goutard had been laying down the law about the technique of street fighting, and incidentally ensuring that my bad dreams would be worse than usual that night. He was going on with relish in praise of concussion grenades when Ruys interrupted.

"If what Major Kinck says is true," he said in his deliberate way, "that sort of fighting is unlikely to be necessary."

"I've found it always pays to expect the unexpected." A typical Goutard discussion-ending pronouncement.

There was silence while we got undressed. Then, as Ruys started to get into bed, he paused and glanced at us reflectively.

"Speaking of pay," he said, "I wonder what this American–West German consortium would give to know what we know."

Goutard pretended to look startled. "Careful, careful!" he warned playfully. "That sort of talk could be dangerous."

Ruys shrugged. "Kinck is no fool. He knows we would think of it. He must be very sure that he has us by the balls." He shrugged again and finished getting into bed. Soon he was quietly snoring.

It was a long time before I got to sleep. First Goutard had made me feel queasy, then Ruys had disconcerted me. He was right about one thing, of course; every man there must have thought about the value of what we knew to the UMAD consortium in Ugazi. The thing that surprised me was that Ruys had not kept such thoughts to himself. I mean I'm just not used to dealing with people who say what they think on delicate subjects like that. I wondered if he were possibly a bit stupid.

The only other explanation could be that he had been putting up a trial balloon because he needed the help of a partner.

In the end I decided that it must have been stupidity. Kinck indeed had us by the balls, and the only contacts we would have with Ugazi, as far as I could see, would be those he had prescribed. Selling out to UMAD was a nice idea—there was a fortune to be had if you could play your cards right—but you didn't need a partner to help you. What you needed was a safe escape route and the nerve to use it.

It was all too well aware that I had neither.

6.

Next morning we paraded in the SMMAC clothing store and were issued with our uniforms.

These turned out to be khaki drill slacks and bush shirts with large pockets of the type Kinck already wore. We were given three sets apiece. There were no badges of rank or insignia of any kind on the shirts. The caps were also of drill, with wide floppy brims. None of it looked very soldierly to me but it was as comfortable as any clothing could be in that heat. There were ankle boots, too, with thick canvas tops and rubber soles, and camp beds with mosquito nets in plastic-coated bags said to be proof against damp and mildew. We had to sign for all this.

Most of the slacks needed alteration. The Indian storekeeper, who had an old treadle sewing machine, took our measurements and promised to deliver everything to the guest house later that day. Then we reported back to the administration compound, where we were each photographed in one of those contraptions like they have in police stations which puts your name in block letters across your chest. These photographs were for our SMMAC identity cards, which Kinck gave to us in the afternoon. He also gave us each a round enameled-metal badge. The enameling was in the Mahindi national colors and portrayed the flag of the republic rippling in a breeze above crossed bunches of corn. This was encircled by the words "One Country, One People" in French and Arabic.

"That badge when worn on the right breast," Kinck told us, "identifies you as an officer in the Mahindi armed forces and senior to any police or other local official. It should under no circumstances be worn or displayed here in Kawaida. It is for use solely in the staging and operational areas."

Barrière held his badge up and examined it critically. "Have you got any more of these, Major?" he asked.

"Why?"

"My wife'll want this as a brooch."

Kinck stiffened. "I hope you are not serious, Barrière. The Fulani are very sensitive. They would consider themselves deeply insulted by the sight of a woman wearing an officer's badge. While on that subject I should perhaps mention to you and Willens that in the staging-area camp it will be better if your wives do not wear trousers."

Barrière merely shrugged, but Willens looked annoyed. "I'll tell my wife," he said, "but I don't think she'll like it. We've seen a lot of Africa and African bush. She's never been instructed about what she has to wear before."

"I am not instructing, only advising."

"You'd be surprised, Major, how well my wife can take care of herself. Any black boy who gets too sensitive with her is likely to end up in small pieces."

"I am glad to hear it."

No more was said about women in trousers, but it was clear that Major Kinck was beginning to get on Willens' nerves. He was already on mine.

We left early the following morning for the staging area, again sitting on the arms and ammunition in the back of the truck, but this time wearing our uniforms.

For several kilometers outside the SMMAC compound the road was tolerable. It ran parallel to and only a short distance from the light railway that carried the ore from the workings in the hills down to Matendo. We passed a Kundi village, the first I had seen. The huts had cone-shaped roofs thatched with leaves and reddish mud walls. They stood well back from the road among tall, flat-topped trees. The men wore short-sleeved smocks, shorts and colored cotton caps. The women's smocks were longer, like big white sacks. They carried their children naked on their hips. There seemed to be a lot of goats.

Just beyond the village the road forked. We turned left toward the railway and almost immediately crossed it. From then on the road deteriorated rapidly. It had been bulldozed fairly recently by the look of it, but rain had carved out deep transverse ruts which reduced the truck's speed to a crawl. It became impossible to sit down. The smaller boxes had begun to slide about with the lurching of the truck. The only thing was to stand up, hold onto the slats and fend off the boxes with our feet. We had half an hour of this torture. Kinck was all right, of course; he was sitting up in front with the driver.

We had been going downhill all this time, but now we leveled off and the road became a little easier again. I say "road," but it was really nothing more than a dark tunnel through the jungle. Tree branches whipped the sides and canvas top of the truck and shut out the sunlight overhead. We were in that stinking twilight for the best part of an hour. When we emerged from it we immediately stopped.

We were in a large flat clearing on the floor of a valley, and there was the railway again. It was a single-track line for most of its length, and this was the place where the empty ore trucks returning from Matendo were shunted around the full ones coming down from Kawaida. As well as the short stretch of double track, there was a siding, a maintenance shed, a concrete house and some thatched huts. A sound of hammering came from the shed. Outside the house stood a jeep and one of those small French cars that look as if they have been built by an amateur mechanic out of scrap—a Citroën 2*cv*. Beside the jeep stood the first Fulani soldier I had seen.

He wore a greasy blue turban, khaki shorts and a webbing belt with ammunition pouches and bayonet frog. He was barefoot, had three vertical scars on each side of his face and looked extremely bad-tempered. He was pointing a bolt-action rifle at us.

A white man in uniform with the officer badge on his shirt came out of the house and bawled at the soldier. The latter looked confused for a moment, was bawled at again and then reluctantly lowered his rifle.

The officer was tall and scraggy with a wiry brown beard and oil stains on his trousers. He gave Kinck a casual salute that was more like a wave of greeting and climbed into the jeep. When he drove off, the truck followed him.

We went down a steep track that led away from the railway. About four hundred meters away there was another clearing and another scowling sentry with scarred cheeks to be passed. We stopped on the edge of the clearing by some of those flat-topped trees. Under them, in the shade, were more huts and two or three store tents.

Goutard took out his officer badge and pinned it on his shirt. The others were doing the same.

I got my badge out, too. A moment later I was an officer in the army of the Republic of Mahindi.

Great moment in history! I can't say I felt like cheering, though. I was remembering a saying of my father's: "*Most officers are pricks until you get to know them better. Then you find that some are bigger pricks than others.*"

For once the memory of him brought me no comfort.

Part Four

Spearhead

One

In the next few days I learned a lot.

To begin with I found out what UZI meant.

The Uzi is a submachine gun designed and manufactured in Israel. With the metal butt folded it is 45 centimeters long. With a loaded 25-round magazine attached it weighs 4 kilos. It fires 9 millimeter Parabellum bullets at a rate of 650 a minute, if you can change magazines fast enough. You can't, of course; but you can, if that sort of game amuses you, strip it for cleaning (twelve parts only) and reassemble it in three minutes flat. It is a chubby little brute with a hunched, arrogant look about it. I never liked handling mine even when it was unloaded. *"The soldier has four best friends,"* my father used to say—*"his two feet, his rifle and, if he plays his cards right, the orderly-room clerk."* I suppose I didn't have my Uzi long enough to look upon it as a best friend.

I was grateful to it, though, at the start. It enabled me to conceal my total ignorance of submachine guns. The Uzi is a post-World War II weapon. Captain Troppmann, the officer with the beard who was Kinck's second in command, Kinck himself and Goutard were the only ones there who had seen a Uzi before, so all the rest of us had to be shown how it worked.

Nobody had a revolver or pistol. I was surprised at this. I had remembered that my father, when he became an officer, had always carried a revolver, a big heavy thing in a shiny leather holster fastened to his Sam Browne belt. I thought of asking about this to show that I was on the ball. Luckily Ruys got in first and was badly snubbed by Captain Troppmann. Troppmann came from Alsace, as Kinck did, and had a very sharp, sardonic manner. For the professional soldier, he said, pistols and revolvers had always been fairly useless and now were obsolete. With the Uzi you didn't have to be a good shot; if you wanted to kill, you killed—at up to two hundred meters if you had time to aim and remembered to flip over the back sight—and you could kill without thinking. Then he got quite steamed up. Pistols and re-volvers, he said, were not for soldiers but for policemen and crooks, for film actors and for real-life psychopaths with doubts, conscious or unconscious, about their mas-culinity. Highly educational it was.

I also found out about magungu huts.

In Kundi they are made this way. The men cut down a lot of saplings and construct a frame with a curved top, rather like a parrot's cage. Then the women arrive—the Emir's troops had plenty of camp followers—and start covering the frame with the long, fleshy leaves of the magungu tree. They put the leaves on in rows, overlapping them like tiles on a roof, until the thing looks like an old-fashioned beehive. There is a door but no window spaces. The theory is that the leaves keep the rain out and at the same time allow the breezes in. What happens in practice is that the magungu leaves keep out *some* of the rain and that the breezes, wafted usually in our case from the general direction of the latrines, are accompanied by swarms of insects. Tree rats and snakes like magungu, too. A black mamba was spotted one day taking its ease in the roof of the European women's latrine. A soldier killed the mamba before it could kill any of us, and Troppmann made a joke of the whole thing, saying that there was nothing like that sort of occurrence for keeping down the incidence of dysentery. Personally I found it no laughing matter. The European men's latrine—a disgusting, pole-over-the-pit affair which I loathed anyway—also had a magunga roof and it was a great strain to have to look up all the time while you were using the place.

There were five European women with us now—five, that is, if you included Captain Troppmann's wife, who was really Eurasian. She was quite attractive and spoke very good French, but she was inclined to be bossy. A lot of Eurasian women I have met are like that. Barbara Willens didn't get on at all well with her. The women had naturally taken charge of the temporary messing arrangements for the European officers, and Madame Troppmann, as the "senior" wife presumably, took it on herself to give the other wives orders. Another source of friction, I think, was the fact that Kinck and the Tropp-

manns were sleeping in the house by the railway instead
of in huts like the rest of us. There was quite a bit of talk
about that.

I took no sides. It was all very well for the Barrières
and the Willens to console one another with the thought
that the present situation was only going to last for a
couple of weeks and that then everything would be
different. I didn't want it to be different. At least, I
wanted it to be different up to a point—the point of getting out of that lousy camp—but I didn't at all want
what would come next.

I had found out what would be expected of me.

Goutard and the others had soon discovered that the
Emir's "battalion" had a strength of less than four hundred men, whose musketry training in most cases had not
progressed much beyond the stage of loading and firing.
They had had little or no target practice. They were,
however, all dangerously trigger-happy. As Willens remarked sourly, they constituted a menace to everyone
except an enemy.

Kinck brushed aside the criticism. "Most of them are
more effective with the bayonet than the rifle," he con-
ceded, "but they will fight if you show them the enemy.
As for the firepower you may need, that is in you gentlemen's hands."

We were all sitting round the food-spotted trestle
table of the mess tent on the morning of the second day.
He went on to explain the mechanics of the expedition.

"The ostensible purpose of our concentration here,"
he said, "is to protect the railway against attempts at sab-

otage. Needless to say—" he gave us the smile—"there have been no such attempts, but our tactical training exercises have been in the form of double envelopments using the railway as an axis. Later, of course, our axis will be the river road to Amari."

He motioned to Troppmann, who proceeded to distribute copies of the secret map of Zone A that had been so hush-hush at Kawaida.

For security reasons—my own security, that is—I don't intend to reproduce it here exactly as it was; but if I am to make people understand the mess I was in and the really appalling dangers I had to face, some sort of map is necessary. If there were any justice in the world it would be drawn in blood supplied by SMMAC's stinking board of directors.

"We shall cross the frontier just north of Matendo," Kinck announced. "There is a Ugazi road block and customs post there but it is lightly held and you should have no difficulty with it. From there you will push on swiftly along the river road. Points at which resistance is encountered that cannot be promptly overcome will be bypassed by the reconnaissance groups and left to be dealt with by the main body. Speed is essential. We must use our advantage of surprise. We cannot allow Amari to be reinforced from across the river. If we cannot seize the town itself on the first day we must at least invest it effectively. The reconnaissance groups must be prepared to cut their way through quickly and ruthlessly."

He flattened one hand and stabbed it across the table at us to show what he meant by ruthlessly. He looked and

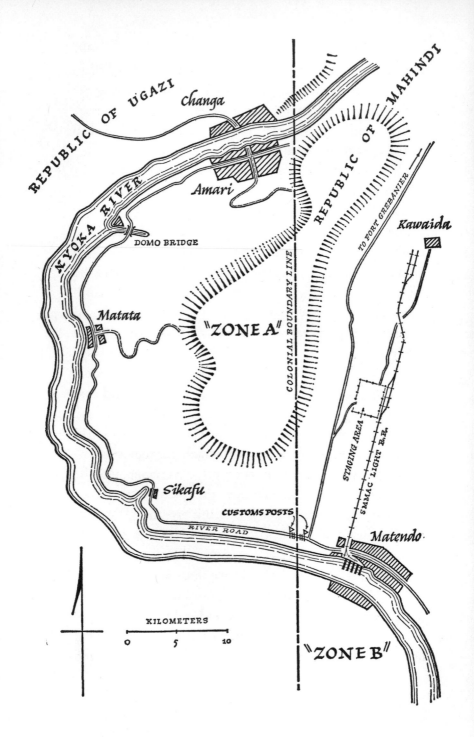

REPUBLIC OF UGAZI

Changa

REPUBLIC OF MAHINDI

NYOKA RIVER

Amari

DOMO BRIDGE

Kawaida

TO FORT GREBANIER

Matata

"ZONE A"

COLONIAL BOUNDARY LINE

STAGING AREA

SMMAC LIGHT R.R.

Sikafu

CUSTOMS POSTS

RIVER ROAD

Matendo

KILOMETERS

0   5   10

"ZONE B"

sounded as if he had an armored division at his disposal.

"Some of you have already had your duties assigned to you. Those who joined earlier have naturally had time to establish rapport with the native officers and NCOs under their command, and company training has been proceeding satisfactorily. By next week companies should be up to strength. I have the Emir's positive assurance of that. However, there remains the matter of the spearhead reconnaissance groups. They must now begin their independent training. There will be two groups and the companies will have to supply thirty men for each. And they must be intelligent men, please, not the cretins you would prefer to get rid of."

There were smiles around the table.

"The groups will also need two NCOs apiece. Captain Troppmann will select those in consultation with company commanders. The group commanders will be as follows. Group One, Barrière with Ruys as second in command. Group Two, Goutard with Willens as second in command. The spearhead force as a whole—that is, both groups—will be commanded by Captain Troppmann. Under him, responsible for communications and liaison, will be Simpson."

2.

I wasn't too worried at first. Communications and liaison didn't sound particularly dangerous. I saw myself sitting by a field telephone, passing on orders and sticking pins in a map.

Then Kinck began to go into details.

Each group, he said, would have two trucks, three machine guns and two mortars. The officers would have Uzis in addition. Selection and training of men for the mortars and machine guns should begin at once. A special area adjacent to the secondary road had been set aside for tactical training and practice deployments.

"There men we're getting," Barrière asked; "will they include drivers for the trucks?"

Troppmann answered. "There may be one or two who say that they can drive, but I strongly advise you to drive yourselves. We don't want any trucks out of action." He looked at me. "I hope you're a good driver."

"Yes."

"He's a professional," said Goutard, rather unnecessarily, I thought.

"Good." Troppmann grinned. "It wouldn't do for the point of the spearhead to get bent, would it?"

I smiled confidently. The implications of what he had

said didn't sink in for a moment.

Kinck took charge again. "On the subject of communications, I should have said that each group will have short-wave fixed-frequency radio transceivers with a range of up to seven kilometers line of sight. As most of the river road lies across flat country you should have no difficulty in keeping in touch with one another."

"How do we keep in touch with the main body?" Willens asked.

"Via Simpson. The spearhead command truck will have equipment of the necessary power. In fact it may be as well for us to begin using our radio code names now so as to get accustomed to them." He glanced down at his notes. "Captain Troppmann and Simpson will be Spearhead, Group One will be Hammer, Group Two will be Anvil. As force commander and leader of the main body I will be Armorer." He looked at Troppmann. "Is there anything else?"

Troppmann shook his head and got to his feet. "No, that is everything. Let's get to work."

He took us first, crammed into his jeep, to the transport park off the road below the camp. It was under heavy guard and there was the usual shouting at and cursing of sentries before we could get through. The guard was commanded by Sergeant Musa, a huge jet-black man wearing a brassard to show his rank and armed with a rhinoceros-hide stick. We were each identified to him and he was told which trucks were now in our charge. We inspected the trucks. The four group trucks were three-tonners with the slatted sides I knew so well by now. The SMMAC lettering on the sides had been painted over but still showed through faintly. The "command" truck was smaller, more like one of the fifteen-hundredweight Guys that the British Army had used in Egypt during the war. It had a canvas top with roll-up sides and a wide box had been built immediately behind the cab. This, Troppmann explained, had been put in to house the intermediate-range radio equipment and its motor generator. Sticking out from the passenger side of the cab was a heavy steel bracket which also looked like a recent addition. Troppmann seemed surprised when I asked what it was for.

"That's where you mount the MAG, of course. The Uzi is a handy little arm, but we need something that can hit at a distance too."

We returned to the camp and went to the main store tent. There we were shown the radio equipment we would have to use—mostly walkie-talkies plus the intermediate-range transceiver that would go in the back of the command truck.

Troppmann was showing me how the latter worked when Willens wandered over and began to ask questions about it. How many frequencies could it handle? What were they? Which one would we be using?

Remembering that he had once been an air-force pilot, I assumed that his interest in the set harked back to those days. Troppmann appeared to make the same assumption and he answered Willens' questions civilly enough; but later, while the MAGs were being uncrated, he took me aside.

"One thing I wish to impress on you, Simpson," he said. "Nobody, positively nobody, is to have access to that intermediate-range equipment except Major Kinck, myself and, when we become operational, you. That is an order. Do you understand?"

"Of course. Is it safe here in the store?"

"For the present. The crystal oscillators have been removed. But we shall want to use it in training soon. Then different precautions will become necessary. You will be told. This is just a preliminary warning."

"I understand."

I did, too. Anyone who knew how to operate that set could make nonsense of Kinck's security blackout if he wanted to—and if he knew whom to contact. But I didn't give it serious thought. I had too many other things on my mind, including, at that moment, the machine gun that Goutard was lovingly lifting out of its box.

The MAG is a Belgian gun designed for the standard NATO cartridge and 7.62-mm. bullet. By adjusting the gas regulator you can boost its rate of fire to as much as a thousand rounds a minute. It is link-belt fed. With the MAG you can kill or wound people a thousand meters away with no trouble at all.

Goutard and Barrière were like children, snapping and clacking the mechanism, showing each other how quickly they could change barrels. I pretended to be intent on studying the radio-equipment instruction manuals. The manuals made no sense at all to me, but then I wasn't trying to make sense of them; what I was trying to think of was a way out of the mess I was in. For a moment, when Willens seemed so interested in the big radio, I had thought of trying to swap jobs with him on the grounds that he was more knowledgeable on the subject. But that, I realized, could get me into an even worse mess. Exchanging Spearhead for Anvil simply meant exchanging Troppmann for Goutard, and the command truck for a three-tonner loaded with mortars and a bunch of murderous *macaques*.

I don't want to give the wrong impression. I'm not a complete coward. I can be brave as the next man when it is necessary to be brave. I mean if the British had called me up in Egypt and sent me off to drive a staff car in the Western Desert I expect I would have gone. I'd have tried to get out of it naturally; the British had plenty of men without picking on me; but *someone* had to stop the Afrika Korps getting to Cairo. I know; I was in Cairo and I felt quite strongly about it.

However, this attack on Zone A was altogether different. *We* were the aggressors. If the Ugazis had been getting ready to attack us I would probably have been very pleased that we had machine guns to stop them with. They would have been sticking their necks out. Instead, it was I who was being asked to stick my neck out. It just wasn't good enough. It was also unethical.

I tried to think of a way of putting the problem to Goutard, but couldn't. He wasn't interested in ethics. Besides, he had started calling me "Spearhead," a piece of facetiousness that naturally irritated me, though I didn't let him see that it did. He was getting back at me, of course. He couldn't bear the thought that, as the officer commanding Group Two, there might come a moment when he would have to take Troppmann's orders from me. The Old Man didn't take orders from Sinbad.

All the same he was a professional soldier and must, I thought, know the score. In our hut that night I tried to find out how he estimated our chances. If he, with his experience, really believed that we were going to be able to bull our way across the frontier and drive eighty kilometers to Amari without getting hurt and without having to do anything more strenuous than accept a surrender when we got there, I wouldn't have much to worry about.

He liked being consulted. He thought about it before he answered, his eyes on the insects swirling suicidally around the Coleman lamp.

"Well, Spearhead," he said finally, "you're the intelligence officer. You tell *me* something. How good is Kinck's information about the Ugazi forces in Amari?"

"Since he bases his whole plan on it, he must believe that it is reasonably good."

"How up to date is it?"

"I don't know."

"Well there you are. His plan relies on there being no change of strength in Amari. If there is no change, then it's easy. We could do it with a quarter the force we have. What I don't like is this waiting. We won't train these imbeciles in two weeks. In two years you might do something. Notice how many carry knives? They like knives. In two years you could work them up the way we worked up the Goumiers in Algeria. Now they're just for show. *Macaques* playing at soldiers. If we're going to be unopposed we might as well forget the main body, load the trucks tomorrow, start driving and get the job over with. By waiting until the main body's up to strength we merely give the enemy more time to find out about us accidentally, more time for him to change his mind about reinforcing Amari. Every day we wait increases our chances of having an opposition to deal with without increasing our ability to deal with it."

"Kinck must realize that."

"He probably does. I'd say he can't do anything about it. He's got to wait until we're up to strength."

"Why?"

"SMMAC may be paying him, and us, but it's this Emir who is in command. It's his operation, not ours, and that's the way it's got to look to the outside world. SMMAC has to keep its hands clean. I'll make a bet with you, Spearhead."

"Yes?"

"We, the whites, may take Amari—for all practical purposes, I mean—but it'll be the blacks under their own officers who'll occupy it."

"I see what you mean."

"And I'll tell you something else. When we take it, *if* we take it, we'd better be prepared to hold on fast to the automatic weapons. If these monkeys get their hands on those, our paybooks aren't going to be much use to us."

"I expect you're right."

"I know I am." His bed creaked as he turned onto his

side. "Don't forget to put the lamp out."

He could have turned it out himself; but no, I was the one who had to reach out from under my mosquito net.

I lay awake in the darkness for a long time. It was like going to school when you haven't done your homework and have run out of excuses. Can you pretend to be taken ill or are you going to be caned? I don't know which is worse when you're dreading the future—to know too little or to know too much.

3.

I learned how to load and fire the Uzi.

I learned how to load and fire the MAG.

I learned not to jump too obviously when a mortar shell was fired nearby.

I learned how to yell at Sergeant Musa and the two *macaques* who had been assigned to act as guards for the command truck. I remembered how my father used to be able to yell an order from one side of the parade ground to the other. I patterned my yelling on his. I might not have looked very soldierly but at least I managed to sound it. Troppmann, who yelled a lot himself, seemed satisfied with my performance in that area.

My performance with the radio was less confident. It was one of those things with a "transmit-receive" switch on it. You couldn't use it like a telephone. Every time you finished saying something you had to switch over to "receive" for the reply, and vice versa. It may *sound* simple, but for a man accustomed for years to telephones it was confusing. I would sometimes forget to switch over. Admittedly this could be infuriating for the person at the other end, but I thought Kinck made rather too much of my occasional lapses. After all, I had never claimed to be an experienced radio operator.

Security on the radio had been elaborated by now. For training purposes at close range the sets were operated without aerials, and test conversations were restricted to non-military subjects. When not in use, the truck radio was padlocked in its box and under guard at all times. So was Kinck's set. The walkie-talkies with their limited range were not so strictly guarded, but even so there were solemn warnings about careless talk while using them.

The tactical drill Troppmann had laid down was very simple. Spearhead went first, followed by Hammer (Group One) and Anvil (Group Two) in that order. If Spearhead encountered resistance it would halt, take up a defensive position and deploy Hammer and Anvil. Hammer would make a left outflanking movement, Anvil a right. If the resistance was small and easily overcome that would be that. If the resistance presented difficulties, Spearhead would join either Hammer or Anvil in bypassing it, at the same time reporting back to the advancing main body so that it was prepared to deal with the situation. Spearhead would push on again.

We had been there a week when Troppmann announced that the time had come to reconnoiter our first
obstacle, the Ugazi road block and frontier post on the
river road north of Matendo. Barrière, Ruys, Goutard
and Willens came with us in the command truck. Troppmann told me to drive. This was the first time we had
been all the way down our track to the Matendo road,
and for those in the back it must have been a rough ride.
The Matendo road itself was not too bad, however, and
for about six kilometers I was able to maintain a fair
speed.

We weren't going right up to the frontier post, of
course. A truckful of white Mahindi officers stopping in
full view to give the place the once-over would, to put it
mildly, have aroused comment. Instead, we stopped just
short of the intersection between the Matendo road and
the Mahindi side of the river road and climbed up the
hillside to the left.

There was no track or pathway and it was steep. For
most of the way we had to scramble up on our hands and
knees over the mash of rotting fern and underbrush beneath the trees. Luckily we didn't have far to go. After
about ten minutes of climbing, the hillside leveled off and
it was possible to stand. The others had got there before
me and were surveying the scene below. I was so out of
breath and the sweat running into my eyes was so uncomfortable that I didn't take any interest for a moment
or two. Then I got my breath back, turned and for the
first time saw the Nyoka River.

In the distance it looked more like a vast green lake.

Even from where we stood you could not see the far bank. The near bank, which we could see curving away to the right, had a dark-green border which I learned later was swamp. Away to the left this border narrowed and then disappeared on the outskirts of Matendo. The wake of a ferryboat made a white streak on the green water.

Only a short stretch of the river road was visible; it soon disappeared into the trees, but the road blocks and customs posts were on the visible section. The Mahindi post was about a kilometer from us with the Ugazi post a hundred meters beyond. They looked practically identical except for the color of the barriers.

Troppmann had a pair of binoculars with him. He passed them around so that we could all take a close look.

The Ugazi road block was made up of earth-filled oil drums painted white and placed so that a vehicle had to slow and make two sharp turns in order to get through. In the middle of the block was a counterbalanced red-and-white-striped barrier which could be raised and lowered by hand. The need to turn made it impossible to crash the lowered barrier at speed from either direction. If Spearhead wanted to get through intact it would have to gain control of the post first.

This was a whitewashed cement-block building with a magungu roof and a bracket with two phone-line insulators on one corner. A khaki-uniformed Ugazi soldier squatted in the shade of what I now knew to be a cassia tree. A rifle was propped against the tree beside him.

"The telephone line connects this post with two of their frontier patrol posts north of here," said Troppmann.

"We shall ignore those, of course, when we go in—they cannot interfere with us—but the second post can communicate with Amari. It is important, therefore, that before taking this post we deal with their telephone."

"One burst from a Uzi will do that," said Goutard; "just blow the insulators off."

"Perhaps," Troppmann replied; "but if we can do this without firing I would prefer it. If *we* start firing *they* will start firing. We don't want any casualties on either side if we can avoid it. Major Kinck and I have worked out a plan on which I should like your opinions."

We waited, all attention. I was feeling better. A war with no casualties would suit me very well too.

"The suggestion is," said Troppmann, "that during the night before the operation begins the Mahindi post should be evacuated by our regular customs personnel and border guards, and that we should take over. The frontier is closed at night. At dawn, Spearhead and Hammer should move their trucks, with troops aboard, fully armed, up to the road block and stop as if they expected to make a conventional border crossing. The Ugazis, of course, seeing the troops, will refuse to let the trucks pass. But there will be arguments, protests and confusion involving, hopefully, all the Ugazi post personnel. Under cover of this disturbance, and moving quietly on foot, Anvil will surround the post, cut the telephone wires and take up covering positions. The post can then be invited to surrender. I would be surprised if they refused the invitation."

Only Barrière had any criticism to offer. "Don't they mount a guard at night?" he asked.

"He will certainly be asleep."

"The two posts are only a hundred meters away. With three trucks arriving and all that unusual activity and monkey chatter going on, he's likely to wake up and wonder what's happening. He could alert the post."

"What is your suggestion?"

"That only one group takes over the Mahindi post—Hammer or Anvil, I don't care which—and let Spearhead and the second group arrive together at dawn to create the diversion. Then it doesn't matter how much noise there is."

"Yes, that is reasonable. Any other points?"

"What do we do with them when they've surrendered?" asked Ruys.

"Leave them for the main body to deal with. They will be close behind us at the start, remember."

It all sounded so easy, so foolproof.

4.

Kinck was away from the camp for the next two days. Officially he had gone to Kawaida; rumor said that he had gone also to Fort Grebanier for a meeting with the Emir, whose promise to reinforce the main body had still not been kept. He returned on the Wednesday with further supplies of mortar ammunition, a case of brandy and new orders.

The orders might have been devised expressly to please

Goutard. They were that we should not wait for further reinforcement of the main body, but proceed immediately with the operation. "Immediately" meant Friday. The Emir had chosen the Muslim holy day to signify that the enterprise had his blessing.

The brandy was welcome.

All we had had to drink in the camp up to that point, not counting boiled water, had been beer. After the canned stew in the mess tent that Wednesday evening everyone began to drink Kinck's brandy. By ten o'clock everyone was reasonably merry, except Adrian Willens. He was pretending to be drunk.

I don't think anyone else spotted the pretense. I had seen him drinking before, it must be remembered, in Djibouti, in Juba and in Kawaida. So had the others, of course, but I am a businessman and in my life I've learned to take careful note of these things. The knowledge of how well or how badly a person holds his drink and the ability to assess the effects of it on his temper and judgment can be critically important in business. As my father used to say, *"If you want to catch 'em with their trousers down, first watch 'em when they're pissed."*

Well, I had watched Willens and he didn't get pissed —not obviously anyway. His face and smile would seem a bit thinner when he'd drunk a lot and his tongue would get a bit sharper and shrewder, but that was all. He was a big, raw-boned man, very calm and casual but with excellent reflexes. I would have said that he could have drunk anyone else there, except possibly Goutard and Kinck, under the table. Yet there he was that evening with a slack grin on his face and nodding idiotically while one of the company officers told him a long, boring story about life in the Congo. I was pretty sure then that he was pretending. When, a little later, he got to his feet, swayed, and then with a muttered apology staggered out of the tent, I was almost certain.

I saw Kinck purse his lips and I caught Barbara Willens' eye. She shrugged slightly.

"My husband's a little out of practice," she said in English.

"Perhaps he has a touch of fever." If he had not been pretending, that might have been the explanation.

She smiled. "Adrian? He's had everything but blackwater, Mr. Simpson. He's immune. Even the mosquitos know it. All he needs is a little air."

She made no attempt to follow him then. At the other end of the table Madame Troppmann was holding forth about the stupidity of African servants, a favorite subject of hers. Mrs. Willens rolled her eyes heavenward.

"Something will have to be done about that woman," she said, again in English. "All these blacky-whiteys are the same. They have to keep on saying how stupid the blacks are because that way they feel whiter."

"I thought she was Eurasian."

"Afro-Eurasian from Guinea. I don't know what the percentages are. I do know that she is a one hundred percent bore. It's going to be purgatory up in that house."

She was referring to the fact that on Friday, D-day, the five women were going to move into the railway house. I didn't attempt to defend Mrs. Troppmann. When people are really *on* about race there's nothing

you can do with them. I was sure Mrs. Willens had me
tapped as a wog and was only tolerating me because I
spoke English. That is why her next remark disconcerted me so much.

"It seems silly to go on calling you Mr. Simpson. It's
Arthur, isn't it?"

"Yes, Mrs. Willens."

"Barbara's my name." She sighed. "I suppose I'd better
see what that husband of mine is up to. Do you mind
walking across to our hut with me, Arthur?"

"Of course not." Their hut was on the other side of
our section of the camp, and in that place walking anywhere after dark could be nerve-wracking; the jungle
was all around you and now and again unpleasant sounds
came from it. All the same I was surprised. We were,
after all, in the European section and there were *macaques* posted to keep the other *macaques* from stealing
our things. And this, too, was a woman who wore trousers and could take care of herself. I was puzzled. I
wasn't fool enough to think that with her husband in the
offing she had any hanky-panky in mind; she'd have
picked on Goutard for that. The only thing I could
think of was that she was tired of speaking French all
the time and wanted to chat for a few minutes in her
own language.

In one way I was right; but only in one way: we had
our chat in English.

As we left the mess tent I got out my flashlight and
switched it on.

"Oh we don't need that," she said.

"I suppose not." The night wasn't pitch-black. You could see the lights of campfires in the company lines twinkling through the trees, and there was a quarter moon.

"Besides, it's easier to talk in the dark."

"Is it? That's a new one on me."

"When you can't see the other person's face and there are just words between you it's only the words that count. You both listen more carefully. Less chance of a misunderstanding."

I was thoroughly confused now. I glanced at her strolling along beside me and could just make out the outline of her face. She was looking straight ahead.

"Adrian isn't really drunk, you know," she said.

"I didn't think he was. I did think that he might be pretending to be."

"That was very sharp of you. Adrian said that you were sharp."

"Not sharp enough to guess why he should pretend, though."

"He's pretending so that you and I can have this talk, alone, without everyone wondering what's going on. They're thinking now that you're just being a helpful little gentleman."

"And I'm not?"

"You could be, Arthur. Helpful to yourself, too. Adrian has a business proposition to put to you."

"That sounds interesting, Mrs. Willens, and I'm listening very carefully, but if your husband has a business proposition to put to me, why isn't he putting it?"

"That's a safety precaution, Arthur. I'm going to explain how that works first, so that you will know exactly where you stand."

"I'm always glad to know that, Mrs. Willens." We had reached their hut now and I slowed down.

"It's all right," she said; "Adrian will stay away until he sees you go back to the mess. We can make ourselves comfortable."

They had two folding canvas stools and we sat down by the hut entrance. She lit a cigarette. The sudden flame of the lighter was dazzling.

"It's like this, Arthur." She clicked the lighter out. "I am going to tell you a secret, and you're going to have to keep it. If you don't, if it shocks you so much that you feel that you have to go running to Mr. Kinck and tell him the terrible thing I've told you, you're going to look a bloody fool."

"I am?"

"Yes, because I'm going to deny having told you any such thing. I'm going to say that you made the story up out of spite and to cover yourself."

"Against what?"

"My husband was drunk and missing. You offered to help me find him. Instead, you made a pass at me. I fought you off and said I would complain to Major Kinck. I didn't. I decided to forgive and forget. But you decided to protect yourself and assuage your wounded pride at the same time. That's why we're here alone, Arthur, so that, if you *do* feel like talking out of school, it'll just be your word against mine."

"I see."

"Which of us do you think would be believed?"

"You've made your point, Mrs. Willens. I think it might be better if you don't tell me this secret of yours." I got to my feet. "I think I'll be safer that way."

She didn't move. "Who wants to be safer? What I'm going to tell you can make you richer."

Now I didn't quite know what to do; I just stood there. Her teeth gleamed in the darkness; she was smiling up at me. "Aren't you even curious, Arthur?"

I hesitated a moment more, then I sat down again. "All right, Mrs. Willens. What's the big secret?"

Although we were still speaking in English, she dropped her voice before she answered.

"Adrian has an old friend in Amari."

"Oh?"

"The friend works for the Ugazi Mining and Development Company—UMAD."

"That's interesting."

"Too right. We ran into him when we were in Entebbe six weeks ago. He's South African, a geologist. I'll call him Bill. Adrian knew him from the war. They were in the air force together. Bill was in Entebbe to pick up some special scientific equipment that had been flown out from West Germany. We were on stopover waiting for a plane connection to Djibouti. Bill spent the evening with us and we all had a few drinks. He talked a bit. He used the phrase 'rare earth' a couple of times. And he gave Adrian his address in Amari."

"Has your husband been in touch with him since?"

"Yes, he has. That's what I'm coming to. We went to Djibouti to join an American who was going into Ethiopia on an animal-collecting expedition. Adrian had been recommended to him as an organizer. Everything was all set and we were getting ready to leave when the American was taken ill with some sort of heart trouble. The whole thing was called off and we were left high and dry. We were getting a bit worried when Kinck approached Adrian with this proposition. It didn't sound bad in Djibouti, did it?"

"No, not too bad."

"Adrian wasn't so sure, though. He's a cautious one. He wired to Bill in Amari outlining the proposition and asking for his opinion. He got a reply the day before we left Djibouti. It was very interesting. Bill knew all about SMMAC, of course. It's a big concern with operations in several of these new countries, and he said they were good for the money. But what Bill wanted to know was *where* the job was. That was very important, he said. And if the job was in Mahindi, Bill said that Adrian must be sure to keep in touch with him. You see what that meant?"

"Yes. He smelled a rat. *Has* your husband been in touch with him again?"

"That's a bloody silly question. How could he have been? That's where you come in." She paused dramatically. "Do you care much who owns this patch of rare earth, Arthur?"

"SMMAC pays me."

"UMAD would pay you more."

"SMMAC is here, UMAD is there."

"Didn't you hear me say that Adrian and Bill were in the air force together?"

"You're thinking of the radio, I suppose."

"Bill said that in the field UMAD used the two-twenty-megacycle band. Adrian says that you have access to that frequency."

"The set may have access to it, Mrs. Willens, but I don't have free access to the set. They're being very careful."

"But you *will* have access to it."

"When we become operational, yes."

"That's what I mean. Now, Adrian has a signal he wants to send. When he approaches you, will you listen to him?"

"I'll listen, but I can't see—"

She silenced me abruptly. "Arthur, until you've listened, of course you can't see. Just remember two things. If SMMAC wins, you'll be paid off when your three months is up and that'll be the end of it. Just another white mercenary looking for a job. If UMAD wins and you are one of those who made the win possible, you could be sitting pretty. Think about it?"

"All right, I'll think, Mrs. Willens." That at least was a promise I would keep.

"Then you'd better go back now. Good night, Arthur."

"Good night, Mrs. Willens."

Goutard looked at me curiously when I returned. As I got myself a much-needed brandy he came over.

"You were gone a long time. Was Willens there?"

"No. We were talking about Australia."

"Is that all? You're losing your touch, Spearhead."

I was tired, I had a lot on my mind and I hadn't at all liked that reference to "white mercenaries." I hadn't seen myself in that light before. For an instant I lost my fear of Goutard.

"Don't call me Spearhead," I snapped.

If I had been feeling better, not so overwrought and confused, I might have enjoyed his look of surprise. It didn't last long, though. A moment later his hard, dangerous look slid into place.

"Getting nervous already, my friend?" His eyes raked me over maliciously. "It's not tomorrow we do the job, you know. You've got a whole day yet to say your prayers in."

"It isn't that," I said instinctively.

"Isn't it? Then it must be something else. Right? Something I don't know about?"

"No."

He went on as if I hadn't spoken. "You don't look yourself, Arthur. I don't think you'd better have any more of that brandy." He reached out and took the glass from my hand. "You've got to keep a clear head. Come on."

I let him take the glass and I let him grip my arm. Then we were outside and walking toward our hut. His fingers were like a vise. We were inside the hut before he let go of me.

"Light the lamp."

I obeyed. He sat on his bed watching me. When the lamp was going he nodded.

"All right. What did you really talk about to the Willens?"

"It was Mrs. Willens. I told you. He wasn't there."

"Go on. We don't have secrets, Arthur. I've told you that before."

So I told him the big secret. It was a relief in a way. As he listened his usual grin came back.

"And you weren't going to tell *me* that?" he asked when I'd done.

"Until I know what Willens has in mind there's nothing much to tell."

"You call that nothing much?" He was behaving very oddly. I had half expected him to yell "treason" and rush off to report to Kinck.

I shrugged. "It makes no sense to me at the moment. Are you going to Kinck? She'll only say I made the whole thing up. I told you that."

"Why should I go to Kinck? Willens is no fool. I should know. He's my second in command. If he's thought of a way of selling out to these UMAD people without risking his own skin, I want to know what it is. If it'll work we may as well share in the profits."

For a cunning man he was very stupid about some things. It irritated me.

"What profits?" I demanded. "How can it work? If he warns this friend of his in time, the Ugazis will be ready for us. They'll put more troops into Amari immediately. If we're still silly enough to try anything, they'll stop us. There may be casualties but there'll be no *coup*. So

UMAD wins and SMMAC loses. What happens then? Willens gets paid off with the rest of us and goes to Amari to contact his friend. What does the friend say? I can guess. 'Thanks very much, old boy, I'm very grateful to you. UMAD is grateful, too. The boss told me to buy you a drink. What'll it be?' End of story. You can't sell information *after* you've given it, when it's public property. That sort of deal has to be made in advance and you have to know whom you're dealing with."

He thought about that for a moment, then nodded. "I suppose you're right. Then what's the game? What's he up to?"

"I'll know better after he's told me about the signal he wants sent, but I'll tell you what I think."

"What?"

"I think that Mrs. Willens told me some of the truth, but I think most of it was half-truth. This old air-force pal of Willens, for instance. He doesn't make sense the way she told it. He may be a geologist but I don't think he was in Entebbe picking up an air shipment of scientific instruments. That was said to make him sound small-fry. I'll bet he's someone pretty high up in UMAD."

"How do you make that out?"

"Mrs. Willens says that he was able to make a deal with the friend from Djibouti by telegram. Could he do that with a geologist who, when he's not working in the field, is used as an errand boy? It makes no sense. There's only one explanation. Willens is under contract to UMAD and has been under contract to them for some time."

"As a spy, you mean?"

"Call it what you like—special investigator, consultant, security adviser. UMAD has a lot to lose. If SMMAC employs Kinck, why shouldn't UMAD employ Willens?"

"But he's an animal collector, a hunter." He was still being stupid.

"No, that's only what he *says* he is." I nearly added that *saying* that I had been an officer in the Eighth Army didn't make it true, but stopped myself in time.

Goutard sighed. "I suppose we'd better tell Kinck."

"Why?"

"Well, if there's no profit in helping Willens . . ."

And then I had one of my ideas.

"There may be no profit but there could be insurance."

He stared.

"Willens is in trouble. He must be or he wouldn't ask me to send this message. Kinck's security has been too good for him. Now he's up against it. Time's running out. He has to take a chance. That means trusting me. He does. He has no choice. He gives me the warning signal to send. I send it."

"You do *what?* They'd be waiting for us!"

I smiled. "If they get it in time. Supposing it gets delayed? We couldn't help it. I did my best—with your help. You see?"

"No."

"A few days ago you were saying that the longer we delayed the greater the risk of our running into opposition. Well, they haven't heard a word from their man

Willens. Supposing they've already done what you suggested they might do. Supposing they decided to reinforce Amari after all. Suppose they're already waiting for us and we're walking into a trap. It would be useful, wouldn't it, if we had something to talk our way out with, if we had a foot in both camps? If SMMAC wins we're on their side, if UMAD wins *we* helped them."

He laughed suddenly and loudly, then reached down into his bag.

"I think you deserve another brandy after all, Arthur," he said jovially.

He produced a bottle.

5.

Thursday was a busy day and Troppmann was in my hair constantly. It was late afternoon before Willens was able to get me alone.

He cornered me finally in the latrine.

"How about taking a walk down the road?" he asked casually.

"All right."

He went out. He was waiting for me on the road near the transport park. He spoke in English.

"There are some rough spots a bit lower down," he said. "We don't want any of the trucks getting stuck in the mud. I thought we might see if it's worth getting a party down to cut brush and fill up some of the holes."

We walked in silence until we were out of sight of the transport park.

"As Barbara explained, there's not a lot to it," he remarked then.

"There's a lot of risk."

"Not if you're careful. My friends over there are monitoring that frequency for ten minutes after every hour twenty-four hours a day. I'll give you their call sign. The moment you get an acknowledgment, which should be within a few seconds, switch back again and read the signal. The whole thing shouldn't take more than two minutes. It's a piece of cake."

"What is the signal?"

"That's in code. Very simple words and in English. You'll have no trouble."

"What do the words mean?"

"They call for an air reconnaissance over what Kinck calls Zone A early tomorrow. They also put Amari on the alert."

"So that they can shoot us up?"

"Don't worry. Spearhead won't get that far. When Kinck sees the planes he'll know he's too late. He'll call it off. SMMAC doesn't want real trouble any more than we do."

" 'We' being UMAD?"

"That's right. Both sides will just pretend it didn't happen. All very civilized."

"Why did you have to leave it so late? What went wrong?"

"I'd counted on my wife remaining a free agent, or fairly free anyway. We've got a man in Fort Grebanier. I was sure she'd be able to get that far. Kinck made the restrictions a bit too tight, that's all. Now it's up to you."

"What's in it for me?"

"A job with us in Amari if you want it. Same pay as this one, but a contract for a year and a bonus of five thousand West German marks payable in advance."

"How far in advance?"

"Well, I don't have the money on me now."

He tried to carry it off with a smile, but it was an uneasy smile. And so it should have been. For running a risk like that he was expecting me to take his word that I would get paid. When I'd said that he was in trouble I had been making the understatement of the year—he was desperate. If I had really been intending to do what he wanted, instead of delaying the signal until it was useless, I'd have laughed in his face.

As it was I merely looked disappointed. "That's not very satisfactory."

"I've written you a personal IOU." He produced a paper from his pocket

"On UMAD paper?"

"Are you crazy? I don't carry that sort of thing on me. Kinck had all our stuff searched in Kawaida. Didn't you know? It was done while they were making out our identity cards. Very careful chap, Kinck. Here." He offered me the IOU and another paper with it. "That's the signal with full instructions what to do. You can't go wrong. The great thing is that it goes off as soon as possible tonight, Arthur. You do understand that, don't you?"

I could feel the tension in him as I took the IOU and the signal. He almost didn't want to let them go. He wanted to be absolutely sure he had me first.

"I'll do my best," I said. "We don't become operational until your group moves out tonight to occupy the customs post. You won't get there until ten o'clock. If Troppmann decides to go with you it should be easy. If he stays behind or if Kinck is hovering around I'll have to wait a bit."

"I realize that. But do your best."

"Of course. There's one other thing, though. I think Goutard is suspicious."

"Why?"

"He's a suspicious type. He saw me talking to your wife. Besides, we've been friends a long time. We share a hut. He knows when I've got something on my mind. He keeps asking questions."

"Can't you put him off?"

"You know him. He's not easy to put off. It might be possible to bring him in, though."

"Would he play?"

"On the same terms?"

"If necessary."

"I don't know. He might. He's not too happy about this set-up. I could put out a feeler."

"For God's sake be careful."

"I'll be careful for my own sake."

"I guess you will. But I'll tell you something. The diffi-

cult part is going to be when Kinck decides to call it off
and pull out. There are going to be a lot of red faces and
itchy trigger fingers around here. We'll have to play it
very straight. We'll have to be browned-off, worried
about the future and sore with Kinck. When they pay us
off we ask for air passage to Entebbe. We go to Amari
from there. You follow?"

"I follow."

"Then we'd better be getting back."

Later in the hut I reported to Goutard and showed
him the IOU. He fingered it greedily. It was made out in
the form of a promissory note, and if it hadn't had my
name on it I think he would have put it in his own
pocket.

"He's ready to do the same for you," I said.

"He'd better be." His grin broadened. "It'll be something for him to do tonight while we're waiting in that
customs post."

My stomach tightened. I had almost forgotten that
within a few hours we would be doing instead of talking.
I forced myself to concentrate.

"The only thing left to decide now," I said, "is when I
do send the signal. Obviously not tonight, but how long
do I leave it tomorrow?"

He thought for a moment and then got out his map.
"Assuming that we have no trouble at the first road
block, we'll be here in this place Sikafu by seven. If we
cut that phone line before they can use it—and I mean to
do that myself—that means no warning will have gone
out by seven. Sikafu is a small place but it might have

a radio. I think we must assume that after seven the news will begin to get through to Amari. In bits, of course, because the monkeys won't be thinking straight. In Amari they'll start running around in circles trying to sort it out. By then we should be in this place Matata, roughly halfway. Reconnaissance planes wouldn't turn Kinck back at that stage. If they started to shoot him up on the road, things might change, but we'll have to chance that. My estimate is that it will take them four hours at least to react at all. You could send the signal any time you get the opportunity after we're through Sikafu. But don't be in too much of a hurry."

"I certainly won't. Don't you worry."

I put some feeling into the words and he grinned at me.

"I won't worry. But what I meant, Arthur, was this. That message is only insurance in case things go wrong. If it looks as though they're going really well it might be better not to send the signal at all. You'll have to decide on your own. Just don't decide too quickly. Decide like a professional. You know."

I nodded. What else could I do? As usual, he made the decisions while I had to carry the can.

"Yes," I said; "I know."

6.

At nine that night we became operational.

As far as Spearhead was concerned that meant that Sergeant Musa mounted the MAG machine gun on the command truck and that Troppmann and I gave the walkie-talkies a final check. Then Troppmann took the padlock off the big radio and connected the long whip aerial. He tested the set and then handed the padlock over to me.

That wasn't, I should add, as much of an act of trust as it may sound. The motor generator which ran the set worked off the truck battery and made a loud whining noise. If I had really wanted to transmit Willens' signal that night I would have had to think up a way of bluffing Sergeant Musa. He was a complete blockhead, of course, but even so it would have been difficult to explain why I had to run the set when I should have been asleep. I was glad that the need didn't arise.

Shortly after nine Goutard and Willens completed the loading of their trucks. Then Kinck arrived and there was a last-minute recap of the orders.

All that Goutard and his group had to do that night was to take over the Mahindi customs post, which had been evacuated for them earlier in the evening. As Willens would have said, that was a piece of cake. But all the same I could feel the tension rising—just my own tension probably, but I thought I sensed it in the others too. Barbara Willens was there to kiss her husband goodbye. Both of them studiously ignored me.

At a signal from Kinck the two trucks moved off down the secondary road. They had their headlights on and we stood watching them until they were out of sight among the trees. Then Kinck came with Troppmann and me to the command truck and I switched on the walkie-talkie.

After about ten minutes Goutard's voice squawked out of the speaker.

"Anvil to Spearhead."

"Go ahead, Anvil."

"Am turning on to Matendo road."

"Okay."

Twenty minutes went by.

"Anvil to Spearhead." Goutard's voice was faint this time.

"Go ahead, Anvil."

"Approaching objective. Lights out."

"Okay."

"No further reports. See you later. Out."

I switched off the walkie-talkie.

We had gone to war.

Part Five

A Day of Battle

One

In Kundi the two hours before dawn are the most tolerable of the day. It is cooler then than at any other time. The nocturnal insects are either gorged or tired and the diurnal varieties are not yet active. Sometimes a light breeze blows and then even the smells let up for a while. You feel that it is safe to breathe.

It was like that when we prepared to move the following morning. If my heart had not been thumping so unpleasantly I would have felt almost human.

Everything but the officers' beds and haversacks had been packed the previous day, so, although it was very dark, the trucks were soon loaded and ready to go. In addition to our weapons and equipment we had ammunition, cans of boiled water, rations for twenty-four hours and emergency medical supplies.

At breakfast in the mess tent we found that we had been joined by the doctor from Kawaida. He would travel with the main body. He was a youngish man with thin lips and a jocular tone. He said that he was there to pick up the pieces and begged us waggishly not to make too much work for him. His obvious enjoyment of the situation got on my nerves.

I had Barbara Willens to contend with too. I had purposely avoided sitting anywhere near her because I knew that she wanted to know if I had sent the signal. As it was she kept trying to catch my eye. Eventually I gave her a noncommittal smile. If she chose to interpret it as a reassuring one, that was her affair. I didn't want to tell her in words that I had already sent the signal. It's silly to tell a direct lie when there's a chance of your being caught out later.

I finished my breakfast, went back to the vehicle park and made Sergeant Musa check through the load again. By keeping busy I thought that I could take my mind off things. As a result the command truck was on the road and ready to go before anyone else. Troppmann was pleased, but it meant that we had to wait.

The order we were leaving in was this. First Troppmann in his jeep, then me driving the command truck with Sergeant Musa on the machine gun and our two *macaques* in the back. Following me would be the trucks of Barrière's Hammer group. Five minutes behind them would be the leading trucks of the main body. That interval would be maintained until we got to the river road. After that, Spearhead and the reconnaissance groups would push on ahead.

Our intention was to reach the Mahindi road block just before first light. At five-thirty exactly Kinck gave the signal and we began to move.

I had my walkie-talkie on the seat beside me and as I turned onto the Matendo road I switched on. A few minutes later I began calling.

"Spearhead to Anvil."

Goutard's voice answered. "Go ahead, Spearhead."

"On Matendo road and approaching. With you in about ten minutes."

Troppmann's voice cut in. "Everything okay, Anvil?"

"Okay and ready to move. No signs of life yet from the other side."

"Good. Are you showing lights?"

"No."

"You'll see ours soon."

Troppmann, ahead of me, put on speed.

A few minutes later I recognized the place where we had stopped when we had reconnoitered the road blocks and knew that we were nearly there.

The road curved slightly and then I saw the intersection immediately ahead. Troppmann turned sharp right and I followed. Barrière and Ruys had closed up now and were right behind me.

This part of the river road was dead straight and I saw the Mahindi block in Troppmann's headlights about two hundred meters before I came to it. Goutard's trucks were parked off to the right under some trees. As we approached, the barrier in the center was raised. I didn't see who raised it. Troppmann's jeep snaked its way around the painted oil drums without difficulty. I had to take it more slowly and the big trucks behind were slower still. This had been anticipated and Troppmann was waiting for us on the far side. The idea was that we should all arrive at the Ugazi post simultaneously with horns sounding and everyone making as much noise as he could.

That part of it worked all right.

As Ruys's truck cleared the road block, Troppmann accelerated and began to sound his horn. That was the signal. We roared up to the Ugazi post and stopped with a screech of brakes and horns all blaring together.

If I had been in that Ugazi post I would have thought the world was coming to an end and stayed inside. If I had been the sentry on duty and that noise had woken me up I would have run for cover.

However, I am not a Ugazi.

What the sentry did was snatch up his rifle, run into the roadway and start shooting at the nearest truck.

As Troppmann had driven his jeep forward into the road block and up to the barrier, the nearest truck on the road was mine.

He got off one shot, which smashed one of the rear-view mirrors, and was working the bolt to get off a second when Sergeant Musa opened fire with the machine gun.

I have never seen a man killed like that before. It was as if he'd been hit by a huge fist which lifted him off his feet and sent him flying backward onto the road.

That was the moment when the men in the post began stumbling out.

As Sergeant Musa swung the gun toward them I yelled at him not to fire again. Miraculously he didn't, but someone else did. From the right came a burst of Uzi fire and a man in the post doorway sank to his knees.

Suddenly it was over. The horns had stopped bleating and I could hear a man inside the post yelling something in a language I didn't understand. Then Willens was there yelling back at him, and Goutard, his Uzi cradled on his right arm, was walking along the side of the road to Troppmann's jeep.

It seemed safe for me then to get out.

Willens and two of his *macaques* were herding the prisoners out of the post. I joined Troppmann and Goutard.

"The line's cut," Goutard was saying. "Shall I wreck the instrument, too?"

"No, we might have a use for that later." Troppmann saw me. "Was that you who opened fire, Simpson?"

"Sergeant Musa did. The sentry started firing at us."

"Any damage?"

"Nothing much."

"Tell Kinck what's happened. Two killed, the rest prisoners. No casualties on our side. His leading truck should be here in a minute. Then let's get moving."

In fact the leading truck of the main body was already approaching the Mahindi road block.

I tried not to see the bloody mess on the road as I went back to the command truck; but I couldn't help seeing, and suddenly the reaction set in. Sergeant Musa was standing there thumping his chest and telling everyone what a fine shot he was. I wanted to yell at him to shut up, but couldn't. It was all I could do to fumble my way back into the cab.

By the time I had made my report there was a pearly pink glow in the sky behind us, and then the sun came up. I was grateful for it. The new day seemed to blot out what had just happened in the headlights and the darkness. I wished, though, that I could stop my legs trembling.

The barrier was raised and we drove through the road block into the Republic of Ugazi.

2.

We reached Sikafu just after seven.

Nothing happened on the way there. We passed through a couple of villages which weren't marked on the map, and the people in them stopped what they were doing and turned to stare at us. They looked exactly like the villagers on the Mahindi side of the border. Kinck had said that they would be friendly. They didn't appear to me to be friendly or unfriendly, just mildly surprised. The goats ignored us completely.

Sikafu is at the head of an inlet separating two stretches of swampland and is where the fishing boats on that stretch of the river land their catches. It is a market town and so has a police station. It also has a smell of its own; to the miasma from the surrounding swamplands is added the breath-taking stench of drying fish.

The sun had been up for nearly an hour now, and when we drove in, the market place was already busy. There were only two or three stalls. Most of the produce for sale—vegetables, fruit and, of course, dried fish—was laid out on mats spread in the dust with the vendors squatting beside them. In the middle of it all, on a small wooden platform, stood a barefoot Ugazi policeman wearing shorts and a white topee with a brass spike on top. He had a wooden truncheon.

Nobody really noticed us until Troppmann stopped his jeep and I pulled up behind him. Barrière's truck was just entering the market place when the policeman turned.

He stared at us incredulously. He was a big, shiny man, a Bantu. I saw his eyes go from Troppman to me, to Sergeant Musa and the machine gun, to the truck full of armed men coming up behind. Then his jaw dropped and he froze. Sergeant Musa chuckled.

At that moment a rifle shot rang out. Probably one of Barrière's clots had felt that insufficient attention was being paid to our arrival and decided to remedy the situation. Or the rifle may have been fired accidentally. I don't know where the bullet went. I don't believe it hit anybody, but the effect of the shot was immediate.

Heads turned, somebody screamed, and that started the panic. Suddenly everyone was screaming and yelling and trying to get out of the market place. Some of the vendors flung themselves on their faces and began to crawl away; others were groveling in the dust trying to salvage their goods as they went. One of the stalls was

knocked over. I saw an old woman in a burka go down
with it.

Only the policeman remained still, staring at us from
his platform as if unaware of the pandemonium.

Troppmann beckoned to him.

The man got down from the platform, stumbled on a
scattered pile of vegetables and came over.

Troppmann had to shout to make himself heard. He
said something to him that sounded like, "*Polisi iko
wapi?*"

The policeman pointed dazedly to the other end of the
market place.

Troppmann motioned him to go ahead.

The policeman began to walk in the direction he had
pointed. Troppmann put the jeep in gear and we began
to follow. Beyond the market place there was the waterfront and some ramshackle wooden houses thatched with
reeds. A big dredger was anchored in the inlet with a tug
alongside it.

The police station was made of mud bricks and had a
corrugated iron roof. The window spaces had heavy
wire netting over them. As we approached, another policeman, wearing a flat-topped cap, came out surrounded
by a group of shouting, gesticulating men who broke and
ran when they saw us coming. Flat-top, who would have
liked to run too, hesitated, then threw up his hands and
awaited his fate.

Troppmann picked up his Uzi, got out of the jeep and
waved me to follow him. When I reached him he was
shepherding the two policemen inside.

The station consisted of one large room, part of which was partitioned off with wire netting to make a lockup. In the other part was a battered table, three chairs, an old wardrobe and a bicycle.

Troppmann asked a sharp question. The second policeman unlocked the wardrobe and brought out a rusty shotgun and an army rifle. He was ordered to put them on the table. There were some further questions and answers neither of which I understood, except for the word *telephoni*, which was used several times. Finally, Troppmann took the bolt from the rifle and we left.

"They say that there's no telephone here," he said as we walked back to the vehicles. "If they want to contact Amari they have to send a bicycle messenger to Matata." He stopped by his jeep and looked thoughtfully at the dredger. "I wonder if that thing has any sort of radio."

There was clothing hanging out to dry on the tug. "If the tug's crew live on board," I said, "they'd have to have some way of communicating with the shore."

"It would take too long to find out now. We'll have to chance it. Report to Kinck and let's get moving again."

For the first time that day I used the big transceiver.

"Spearhead to Armorer. First objective secured. Now preparing to move on. Over."

"Armorer to Spearhead. Any incidents? Over."

"No incidents. Police appear cooperative. Over."

"Very well. Move ahead. Over."

"On our way. Over and out."

I had no opportunity of sending Willens' signal, even if I had wanted one, then. Troppmann was standing by

the truck listening to every word I said. After a brief
local conversation on the walkie-talkies we got on to the
road again.

It was very hot and steamy by now. On our left as we
went there was nothing but swampland and, on our
right, dense jungle. The road had a dirt surface which
Troppmann's jeep churned into a plume of dust. The
dust caked in the sweat. Insofar as I was capable of being
glad about anything at that moment I was glad that I
wasn't riding in one of the trucks behind me. We passed
a bus going in the opposite direction—it had to pull off
the road to let us by—and a few cyclists, but otherwise
there was little traffic.

Matata is on the river road at the junction of the two
roads leading into the interior. This is only a secondary
road giving access to a cocoa-growing area, but in a
country with so few roads a town at a road junction
tends to grow. In colonial days, according to Troppmann, Matata had been a subdistrict headquarters with,
at one time, as many as thirty Europeans living on the
plantations in the nearby foothills.

The jungle thinned and it became possible to glimpse
the hills and mountains of the interior far away to the
right. We passed through a small village. Then, for about
a kilometer, the road was slightly uphill. From the top of
the rise we could see the roofs of Matata and the curve in
the river line which showed on the map.

A short downhill stretch followed and then we were
on the level driving past a row of cocoa fermentation
sheds. There was a bend ahead and a traffic sign with the

words NJIA ZAPITANA on it. I didn't know what that meant.

The first indication I had that there was something wrong came when Troppmann, who was just entering the bend, suddenly slammed on his brakes, wrenched the jeep off the road and backed quickly. At the same moment there was a sound of firing.

I turned off the road, stopped and switched on the walkie-talkie. A moment later Troppmann's voice came over.

"Spearhead to Hammer and Anvil. Stop and await orders. There's a road block ahead. We will reconnoiter and decide how we deal with it. You get that?"

As Barrière and Goutard acknowledged, I saw Troppmann waving to me to join him. I picked up my Uzi and got down. My legs felt most peculiar, almost as if they didn't belong to me, but I walked along the shoulder of the road to the jeep as he jumped out of it.

"Someone's given them the news," he said. "It can't be helped. We've not far to go now."

"What sort of a road block is it?"

"You'll see in a minute."

He began pushing his way through the undergrowth in a direction parallel to the road. I followed him like this for about fifty meters, then he began to ease slowly to the left—that is, toward the middle of the bend. As he moved forward now he went into a crouch. I did the same.

When we were almost on the road again he stopped and peered through the leaves. I came up beside him.

I could see along the road now. The road block was about two hundred meters away and consisted of a bus like the one we had passed earlier. It had been driven broadside across the road at a point where there were trees on both verges. There was no way of driving around the bus; the trees would prevent that. If we were to go on at all the bus would have to be moved.

Troppmann crouched a little lower, unslung his Uzi and pulled back the cocking handle. Then he pushed the change lever forward to "automatic."

"Let's find out what they've got there," he said. "You watch the left side."

He raised the gun to his shoulder, leaned forward slightly and fired three quick bursts, one to the left of the bus, one at the bus and one to the right of it.

Though the din made me flinch I kept my eyes open and saw the leaves and dust spurt up as the bullets tore into the bushes. I also caught a glimpse of a man moving quickly to take cover behind a tree.

My ears were still singing when the reply came, a ragged burst of rifle fire. It didn't seem to be aimed at us but it made a lot of noise. I saw one of the bushes move as the firing ceased.

Troppmann eased back and sat on his heels.

"What did you see?"

"There are some men on the left among the bushes. One's behind that big tree."

"They fired about a dozen shots. That's probably how many there are of them. This'll be quick and easy."

We went back the way we came. Personally, I didn't

see how it could be either quick or easy. If the trucks
came on down the road, they would get bullets in their
radiators and the drivers would get bullets in their heads.
If the men came on without the trucks, they would be
picked off as soon as they showed themselves. If they
were going to have to work their way around on the
flanks as they had been taught, we would be there all
day.

As soon as we got back to the jeep Troppmann started
giving orders.

To me he said: "Contact Kinck. Report the situation.
Tell him that we'll be a few minutes cleaning this up.
Send Sergeant Musa to me."

Then he picked up the walkie-talkie and called Barrière. I didn't wait to hear what he said. The time had
come, I had decided, to send Willens' signal and now I
had the opportunity.

I got up into the back and told the two *macaques* there
to get out and stand guard.

First I reached Kinck and told him exactly what
Troppmann had said without mentioning my misgiv-
ings about the situation. Kinck seemed to have no mis-
givings of his own. He said calmly that the main body
was about to leave Sikafu and told me to report again
when the road block was cleared.

It was exactly three minutes past ten by my watch.

The moment he said "over and out" I turned the frequency selector to two-twenty megacycles. Nobody was
paying any attention to me. My two *macaques* were
watching Barrière's men unloading something from his

truck farther up the road. I got Willens' signal out of
my pocket.

All I had to do was say "Janson Two, over" and
switch to receive. I did this three times before I got a
reply. When it came it was very loud and clear.

"Janson Two listening. You're coming in strength
five. Go ahead. Over." The voice spoke in English with
an accent like Willens'.

I switched over and read the signal. It began: "Immediate, Executive from Fielder." The rest was in code
words which made no sense.

When I had finished I said "over" and the voice read
the message back. "That right?" he concluded.

"That's right. Over."

"Left it a bit late, haven't you, Fielder? Over."

"This isn't Fielder. You've got the bloody message.
The rest's up to you."

"Who's that talking?"

I told him to go and bugger himself and switched off. I
was sweating and shaking so much that my fingers
slipped on the switch. That was lucky in a way because it
reminded me to turn the frequency selector back to the
band Kinck was using.

My hand was still on the set when there was an ear-
splitting bang which made me jump and graze my
knuckles. A mortar had opened fire just up the road from
me. Barrière was in charge of it. A soldier crouched beside him with a walkie-talkie. As I looked around I saw
that Ruys had set up a second mortar beyond. There was
a crash as the mortar shell exploded farther down the
road.

I got back into the front of the truck and switched on my walkie-talkie set. Troppmann had gone back to the place off the road from which we had reconnoitered and was directing the mortar fire.

Barrière and Ruys had lobbed about ten rounds apiece when there was a long burst of Uzi fire from the direction of the block and Troppmann's voice came through saying "That's it, Hammer. Cease fire." Then he actually chuckled. "Bring the truck up, Spearhead."

I drove forward around the bend in the road. Troppmann was standing by the bus watching Sergeant Musa, who was in the driver's seat trying to find out how to start it. There was a dead man with half his head blown off lying to one side. He was in some sort of uniform and his hands still clutched a rifle.

Troppmann changed the magazine on his Uzi. As I stopped by him he tossed the empty one into the back of the truck.

"What happened?" I asked stupidly.

"What do you think?" He grinned. "They found it was no fun being mortared. Those that were left tried to run. We got the lot. Look, you'd better shift this bus out of the way. Musa will take all night. Then report to Kinck. We'll be ready to move again in five minutes."

He walked back up the road to get his jeep.

I did as I was told. From the height of the driver's seat of the bus I could see more of what had been done by the mortar shells. I just tried not to look at it. Mortar shells don't make big craters in the earth but they do horrible things to human beings.

3.

It was ten-thirty when we entered Matata.

The river road was also the main street of the town. It was deserted. Faces peeped at us from the huts and houses as we went by.

Sergeant Musa was offended.

"They are of our people," he grumbled. "They have been told we were coming. They should be welcoming us."

Out of the corner of my eye I could see him fingering the machine gun. Personally, I found Matata's lack of enthusiasm completely understandable. If I had been one of them I wouldn't even have peeped at Sergeant Musa; I would have kept my head down.

Matata had a square in the center like that of a small French provincial town with a stone *mairie* on one side. I expected Troppmann to stop there but he didn't. Presumably he thought that, by killing the men at the road block, he had dealt sufficiently with the local gendarmerie and that now that the news of the invasion was out there was no point in cutting communications.

By eleven we were eighteen kilometers from Amari near a place called Domo. It was there that we ran into our first serious trouble.

Domo is a fishing village on a shallow inlet something like the one at Sikafu, but narrower and longer. It winds inland for about a kilometer and the river road crosses it by means of a concrete bridge.

The presence of the hastily improvised bus road block near Matata suggested that the news of our approach had been radioed ahead from Sikafu. That meant that when we reached the bridge near Domo the authorities in Amari had had less than two hours in which to react. The warning signal I had sent wasn't even an hour old. According to Goutard they should still have been running around in circles trying to decide what, if anything, to do about it. Most of them may have been doing just that; but unfortunately someone there had stopped running long enough to think of sending troops to the bridge before we got there.

As it approached the bridge the road ran absolutely straight for nearly a kilometer. On both sides of it there were cocoa plantations which had gone out of cultivation; that is, the brush had been left to run wild under the trees. As a result you couldn't see what was there. It was an ideal place for an ambush. If they had held their fire a bit longer they could have murdered the lot of us.

Luckily, their *macaques* were as trigger-happy as ours.

Troppmann's jeep got it first. There were two quick bursts of automatic fire and I saw him swerve wildly. For a moment he straightened up, then he ran clean off the road into the undergrowth on the right.

I skidded to a stop, slammed in reverse and accelerated. Goutard's truck was only about seventy meters behind me, and if he hadn't stopped and backed away quickly too I would have hit him. He also had the presence of mind to get off the road. It took me five extra seconds and another burst of fire to decide that off the road was a better place to be than on it just then; but with Sergeant Musa beside me blazing away like a maniac at nothing, it was difficult to think straight.

As soon as I came to a stop I scrambled out and got behind the truck. Along the road a cloud of steam drifting up showed where Troppmann's jeep was. Then I saw him crouching in the bushes behind it. He had his Uzi in his hands and didn't seem to be hurt.

Goutard came up behind me. "Give him covering fire," he snapped; "they're off on the far side there, about three hundred meters."

"They may be on both sides."

"We'll find out soon enough. Let's get him out first."

The command truck had come to rest at an angle which made it impossible to point the MAG down the road, so now it had to be moved. I was just going to move it but Goutard brushed me aside and did it himself. Then he brushed Sergeant Musa aside and took over the gun. A few seconds later it was hammering away and I could see the brush flying where the bullets ripped into it. From farther back two MAGs on the other trucks joined in.

Troppmann began to move toward us, crawling, running and dodging among the bushes on our side of the road. There was so much noise that it was impossible to tell if the enemy were firing at him or not. Anyway they didn't hit him. He got back scratched, breathless and sweating.

Barrière and Willens came up as Goutard got down from the truck.

"Are they on both sides?" Barrière wanted to know.

"Yes, but mostly on the left." Troppmann spat, wiped some blood off his face and began to swear about the loss of the jeep.

Then Willens was beside me muttering urgently in my ear.

"Did you get my signal off?"

"Yes."

"When?"

"Early this morning." I didn't want him to ask how early, so I went on quickly. "Where are those reconnaissance planes you talked about?"

He had no chance to reply. Troppmann had begun issuing orders.

"When you go for them keep moving fast. They're not very deep in. Get near the bridge first before you start mopping up. We'll keep the road covered from here until you're well behind them. Then we'll push forward."

For a while there was comparative quiet as Hammer and Anvil went off on foot into the cocoa trees and began their encircling movements. Then the enemy realized what was happening and began to react. There were distant shouts, then bursts of rifle and automatic fire. I was in the back of the command truck reporting the situation to Kinck when Troppmann, who had taken over the MAG, opened fire on something in the road. The noise so close at hand drowned out my voice. I yelled that I would call later and switched off.

By peering over the top of the box housing the set I could see what was happening.

Just short of the bridge some of the enemy had pushed a small truck out onto the road and were trying to use it as cover to cross from left to right. It wasn't long enough and two of them who had tried were already lying in the road, caught by the MAG. They wore jungle-green uniforms and helmets. One of the helmets had come off and rolled away when its owner had gone down. As I watched, the truck started to move slowly—obviously they were now trying to push it across from the far side —and Troppmann opened fire again.

The bullets were kicking up the dust beneath the truck wheels when suddenly it stopped and then rolled back. Troppmann ceased fire and at that moment the walkie-talkie came to life.

"Anvil to Spearhead. We're in position and covering the bridge." It was Goutard's voice.

Troppmann kept his eyes on the road. "Check with Hammer," he said to me.

But Barrière had heard Goutard's message. "Hammer to Spearhead," he said. "I can't cover the bridge from this side yet. Give me a couple of minutes."

Troppmann nodded. "Tell him that's okay. But we'll get ready to move."

Sergeant Musa and our two *macaques* had been adding to the din with their rifles from positions in the bushes. I yelled at them to get back into the truck and climbed over into the driving seat with the walkie-talkie.

"When we do move we'll move quickly," Troppmann said; "we don't want to get caught in any crossfire." He hesitated, then made up his mind. "In fact I'm not waiting any longer for Hammer. We'll move now."

"Now? Shall I warn the others?" Anything to postpone the evil moment.

"I'll do that. Just stop talking, get going and keep going until you're on the bridge." The loss of his jeep had made him very bad-tempered.

"But . . ."

He looked at me sharply. "Get moving or get out!"

I didn't want to do either; I wanted to do nothing; but in his way Troppmann was as terrifying as Goutard. I put the truck into gear.

At that moment Barrière came through again.

"Hammer to Spearhead. I'm in position."

Troppmann answered. "Spearhead to Hammer and Anvil. Move in. Clean up. Reform at the bridge."

I began to drive again.

It was less than a kilometer to the bridge. At the speed I was going it couldn't have taken more than a minute; but it was a very persistent minute. I passed the shot-up jeep and I passed the truck with the dead men by it. That second bit seemed to take an age because I tried to avoid seeing the bodies and as a result nearly ran over them. The cocoa trees were all around, hemming me in. From them, high-pitched above the racket of the engine and the tearing thumps of concussion grenades, came the snapping and snarling of automatic fire. It felt and sounded as if everyone was firing at me and only me, and if that sounds self-centered I can't help it. I *felt* self-centered, and—to be absolutely frank—soft-centered as well. If I'd had anything to eat since breakfast I would certainly have thrown up. Whether I personally was being aimed at or not, I regard the fact that I reached the bridge without anything actually hitting me as nothing short of a miracle.

As soon as I stopped, Troppmann got out and looked back down the road.

There was still some scattered firing going on and, though the balustrades at the side of the bridge weren't very high, it seemed safer on the ground than sitting up in the truck. I got down and joined him.

"Let's see what's happening," he said, and began to walk back the way we had come. I followed reluctantly. I could guess what was happening and I had seen more than enough already.

On the bank of the inlet we found Goutard and Barrière. They were standing there calmly chatting to a white man in the jungle-green uniform of the enemy. Beyond them, squatting on the ground, were four prisoners guarded by some of Barrière's *macaques*.

As we came up, the strange white man turned, saw Troppmann and gave him a bitter smile.

"Oh, it's you," he said. "I might have known."

Troppmann laughed. "What's the matter, Jean-Pierre? The game getting too rough for you these days?"

"How can you play it with these stupid louts?" Nobody had taken away his submachine gun. He made a gesture of annoyance with it. "We should have made mincemeat of you."

"You were unlucky," Troppmann said graciously. "Our lot are just as bad. Have you boys introduced yourselves? This is Captain Velay, who, for once, has chosen to sit on the wrong side of the table."

Velay nodded to us gloomily as we were introduced. He was a heavy man with broad shoulders, a pink complexion and a long, pointed nose. Two of the fingers of his left hand were missing.

"I don't know what you people think you're up to," he went on. "SMMAC won't like it when we stop the ore barges out of Matendo. That's what'll happen, you know. We can do it easily, sink the lot if necessary. UMAD means business."

"Well, so do we, Jean-Pierre."

Willens arrived at that moment to report somewhat wearily that we had had four casualties, including one dead. The dead one had blown himself up with a grenade.

Willens didn't look at Velay, and Velay appeared not to see Willens; it was pretty obvious that they knew each other. Troppmann didn't seem to notice, however.

"How many men did *you* lose?" he asked Velay.

"Five or six killed, I think. One or two wounded. What are you going to do with those prisoners?"

"What will they do if we turn them loose disarmed?"

"Kill your wounded, I expect, and then walk back to Amari."

"We'll take our wounded with us. You'd better warn your men to lie low and let our main body pass through before they start walking."

Velay shrugged. "Okay. What do *I* do?"

"I'm afraid I'll need your truck, Jean-Pierre. You wrecked my jeep. How about coming with me?"

"Not if you think you're just going to drive straight in. You won't get away with that. I'd sooner walk."

"Where will they try to stop us?"

"At the brewery. And they *can* stop you, believe me. I set it up myself. We have heavy machine guns."

"We have mortars and MAGs."

"It's a ferro-concrete structure."

"Then we'll bypass it."

"You could try." Velay thought for a moment. "If I were doing it I'd forget about the main road and cut across country to the Ebony Road."

"With what object?"

"Have you a map?"

Troppmann produced a map and Velay pointed to the secondary road that ran east of the town for a short way into the hills.

"From there," he explained, "you could enter the town by the Ministry of Agriculture's experimental station and advance about as far as here."

He rested the muzzle of his gun on the map.

"What stops me there?" Troppmann asked.

"The military barracks."

"Thank you very much, old friend. More heavy machine guns?"

"Naturally. But there you are in the town. You have accomplished your mission. Leave the rest to Kinck. He has done no work today."

"I am ordered to invest Amari. You call this investment?"

"Listen, my friend." Velay's tone was restrained and patient. "You don't want casualties, neither do we. You will occupy Amari for a few days, no doubt. But you will certainly be obliged to leave it then. Pressures will be applied, good sense will prevail. Why shouldn't we be sensible now?"

My heart warmed to Velay. That was the kind of talk I liked to hear. I believed that he meant what he said.

To my amazement, Troppmann laughed. "You wouldn't kid an old pal, would you, Jean-Pierre?"

Velay looked slightly offended. "Please yourself," he said huffily; "you asked for my advice."

"I might take it later, but I think we'll have a look at this brewery of yours first."

Velay shrugged as if to wash his hands of the whole affair. I sympathized with him. The limit of my interest in breweries at that moment was that I badly needed a drink.

Troppmann began giving orders again. I, of course, was sent back to the command truck to report to Kinck. On the way there I glanced at my watch.

I thought it must have stopped. The time was only eleven-forty.

4.

The brewery at Amari is the first building of any size that you come to on the outskirts of the town and has a big sign with the words BRASSERIE TEMBO painted in blue on the end wall. It stands where the road divides, one branch going down to the waterfront, where the ebony logs from the hill forests were loaded, the other continuing to the center of the town. In places like Amari the transition from country to town is usually quite sudden. Just before the road divided there was a village of magungu huts on the left, and then you saw the brewery with its painted sign on the right. In that setting it looked utterly incongruous.

Troppmann with Velay beside him in the latter's truck stopped well short of the place where the road divided. If there were heavy machine guns in the brewery, as Velay had said, that would be the area they covered. Troppmann had retrieved his walkie-talkie unharmed from the wrecked jeep and now I heard him calling Barrière.

"Spearhead to Hammer. I want you to send a party forward to draw fire."

"Okay. Who'll cover me?"

"We will. Command truck, follow me."

Sergeant Musa smacked his lips and began loading a fresh belt of ammunition. My stomach heaved.

There was a thin belt of trees on the edge of the village to Troppmann's left and he drove off the road into them. I followed. This was village land and small chickens began running about as we approached. It was necessary to go slowly over that uneven ground, and one of my *macaques* took advantage of the fact to jump down and seize one of the chickens. He didn't kill it then, just tied its legs together with a piece of creeper and threw it squawking into the back of the truck. I wondered if he would live to eat it.

In spite of the trees I was beginning to feel very exposed there. Troppmann was almost level with the intersection of the two roads now and the brewery was less than four hundred meters away and facing us. If we weren't careful, I thought, it would be us who would be drawing fire.

Then Troppmann stopped. I turned the truck a little so that Sergeant Musa could cover the brewery and stopped too. I also got out of the driving seat. Behind the truck was soon going to be a safer place than in it.

Through the trees now I could see Barrière and half a dozen of his men moving up on the brewery side of the road. Where the road divided there was a V-shaped mound covered by bushes. This was the only cover in the intersection. Suddenly Barrière and two other men ran forward into the open, heading for the mound.

There was a burst of fire from the brewery and bullets whacked into the road, but Barrière reached the mound safely. As he crouched down behind it he waved to the other men to join him. They did and again the brewery fired. This time I saw the flashes. So did Sergeant Musa. He gave a yell and began to fire back.

The brewery compound was enclosed by a high metal fence and the fire was coming from two places to the left of the main gate; they were firing through holes in the fence.

And then I had one of my ideas. I remembered what Velay had said when Troppmann had mentioned mortars—that the brewery was a ferro-concrete structure. At the time that had seemed an answer. Now I realized that it wasn't. Concrete is no protection unless you can get behind it. It was obvious, from looking at the windowless façade of the brewery, that if you really wanted to make it a strong point you would have to make loopholes in its walls first. That would take time and there hadn't been that much time.

I went to the walkie-talkie and told Troppmann my idea.

"Amazing!" he said. "Have you just thought of it?" He chuckled fatuously. "I must tell Captain Velay."

Of course, he was trying to pretend that he himself had had the idea all along, but I wasn't deceived. He certainly acted on my suggestion. Ten minutes later mortar shells were blasting the enemy in the brewery compound to bits.

I was sorry about that, naturally, but in war there is no room for sentiment and half measures. As my father used to say, "*The soldier's job is to fight the enemy, not just fart at him.*"

Barrière's group were left to mop up at the brewery while the rest of us pushed on into the town.

When I reported this to Kinck I had some news from him. The main body had been attacked by three planes on the road outside Matata. The planes had come from across the river. There had been no casualties, but "some disorganization of the column" had resulted, and it would be two hours before they caught up with us— more, perhaps, if the air attacks were repeated.

Troppmann pulled a face when I told him.

I could understand why.

When Barrière's group had finished at the brewery they would move down to the waterfront and take over there, or try to. Their orders were to secure the piers, fuel stores and any boats that were still there and stop all movement, in or out, by river. If they had no trouble they could probably do it, but they would have no men to spare. That left only Goutard's group to deal with the barracks and the garrison inside it. That was all right if all the garrison was going to do was defend the barracks compound. But if, when they found that we didn't im- mediately attack it, they decided to come out and attack us before the main body arrived, we would be in a mess.

We had stopped just short of the main square in a tree- lined street of broken-down two-story buildings. Some of them were houses but most were shops, hole-in-the- wall cafés and bars. Groups of black men in European dress stood outside the cafés and stared at us. They didn't seem afraid; some were even laughing and making jokes among themselves; quite a few were very obvi- ously drunk.

There was no feeling now, as there had been in Sikafu and Matata, of our being on top. On the contrary, I felt that we had bitten off more than we could chew, and that at any moment something very unpleasant might happen. It may sound stupid, but, as I stood there waiting for Troppmann to make up his mind what to do, I wouldn't have been at all surprised if policemen had suddenly arrived and arrested the lot of us.

Goutard's group had already gone on ahead to see what the score was at the barracks, and now Troppmann decided to join them.

We turned away from the square and went uphill for a short way past a walled colonial cemetery. Goutard's trucks were parked at the roadside near it.

We parked behind them. As I got out of my truck a plane roared overhead very low and fast. I caught a glimpse of the Ugazi colors on the wings and then it was gone. It didn't drop any bombs. Probably, all the pilot wanted was to see if the Ugazi flag was still flying over the barracks.

It was.

Goutard had his group deployed inside the cemetery behind the crumbling wall facing the barracks. It was necessary, he warned us, to keep our heads down. The garrison had proved to be both alert and jumpy. They had two machine guns set up on the roof and would blaze away instantly at anything they saw moving. The fire wasn't very accurate but accidents could happen. Willens was setting up guns to cover the main gate and the open ground in front of it. With his own guns he proposed to make things dangerous for, and reduce the enthusiasm of, those on the roof. He had a spy hole in the cemetery wall and we took turns peering through.

About two hundred meters away on the far side of a square of dusty wasteland there was a long, high stone wall with an arched gateway in the middle. The building behind it looked rather like a jail. The heads of the machine gunners on the roof were just visible. From the flagstaff above them drooped the green and white Ugazi flag. The fortress-jail effect was relieved only by an enormous scarlet bougainvillea which rioted over the arched gateway and along part of the wall.

Troppmann glanced at Captain Velay. "Who commands the garrison?" he asked.

"Colonel Ngozi."

"Any white officers?"

"No."

"What will he do, Jean-Pierre? Would he attempt a sortie?"

"I doubt it. He will hold out until he gets help from across the river."

"Would he *sell* out?"

"He might." Velay smiled beguilingly. "Would you like me to ask him?"

"That's good of you, Jean-Pierre, but I'd prefer that he doesn't know our strength at the moment. He might decide to break out. Later perhaps, when the main body gets here, you might ask him."

Velay sighed. "My only wish is to be helpful."

"Naturally."

A sound of firing came from the river direction. After a moment or two the sound came again. Troppmann turned to me.

"Go and ask Barrière how he's getting on."

As I crawled away there was more firing. The sound seemed to excite the men on the roof of the barracks. There was a violent hammering noise and broken twigs rained down on me from the trees overhead. I was very glad to get out of the cemetery and back to the truck.

Instead of Barrière I got Ruys. He was very much out of breath.

"A bit of trouble," he said. "There are some men in a building just off the river front on the west corner of the square. I think it's the Prefecture. They have rifles. We are more or less pinned down here. We've tried to outflank them but there's no way. And René has been wounded."

René was Barrière. "Badly?"

"No, but it's a leg wound and he's out of action. We're all right where we are for the moment, but we can't take the ferryboat pier from here. Someone'll have to clear that building from the square side first."

"I'll tell Troppmann."

Reluctantly I went back into the cemetery and told Troppmann. Goutard and Velay were listening as I made my report.

"Those are our men," Velay said quickly. "UMAD personnel. Civilians."

"What are they doing in the Prefecture?" Troppmann demanded.

"What the Prefect and his staff should have been doing if they hadn't escaped across the river when the alarm
was given."

"Are these men Europeans?"

"Two of them are and there are three *évolués*." By
that he meant "civilized" men. The term covered any
African—from a clerk who could just use a typewriter
to a lawyer with a university degree—who wasn't an ordinary *macaque*.

"Can't you tell them to be sensible?"

But Velay had abandoned his pretense of trying to be
helpful. "They *are* being sensible," he said. "You're held
up here. You're held up down there. If Kinck doesn't get
here by tonight you may be on the run by morning.
We are friends, yes, but not at present colleagues. Do
you really expect me to make it easy for you?"

The last remark seemed to anger Goutard. He made
the same gargling noise in his throat which had preceded
his assault on Captain Van Bunnen.

"I'd soon have them out of it," he said.

Troppmann stared at him for a moment. "I can't let
you take any men from here."

"I don't need any from here. There are three on the
command truck and Arthur. If those others only have
rifles and shotguns, that's plenty to do the job."

They both looked at me. Goutard had his pinched
look. I could have screamed, but I couldn't think of anything to say. I shrugged.

Troppmann still looked at me doubtfully, but he
nodded. "Very well. Don't hurt them unless you have to.

I'll tell Ruys that you're on the way."

It was really just as well that one had to crawl to get out of the cemetery safely. I don't think that I could have walked upright.

5.

The main square in Amari has buildings on only three sides. The fourth side is formed by the river front where the bigger passenger launches and ferryboats tie up. On one side there is a church, part of the Catholic mission and a hotel with a big verandah. The other buildings are all provincial government or commercial offices. The patch of ground in the center has a few acacia trees and a stone memorial surrounded by an untidy bed of canna lilies.

Instructed by Goutard, who sat beside me, I drove slowly into the square and then stopped so that he could get his bearings.

There were quite a lot of people there; but, except for some drunks near the memorial, they were congregated on the right side by the church. The Prefecture was the end building on the left side, and the roadway in front of it was empty. If there was going to be any fun the crowd preferred to view it from a distance.

Goutard told me to drive on, keeping to the left, but to

stop again just beyond the main entrance to the Prefecture. I was to go slowly. I did as I was told. I was too
frightened to do anything else.

As we approached, even the drunks by the memorial
decided that it might be wiser to withdraw a little. When
Goutard traversed the MAG menacingly in their direction some of them ran.

The Prefecture was on two floors and overlooked the
river front. Even I could see now that a few determined
men with guns on the upper floor could make things impossible for anyone on the front itself. There was no
cover of any sort there. Barrière would have needed armored cars to get by without casualties.

It seemed to me that we were going to need a tank to
get into the Prefecture itself. All the lower windows
were barred and shuttered. The big double doors in the
entrance portico looked firmly forbidding.

Goutard seemed unimpressed, however. As I stopped,
he picked up the walkie-talkie and called Ruys.

"We're in the square and about to go in."

"Good."

"I'm going to start with grenades. When you hear
them I want you to keep those types upstairs busy. I
don't want them crossing over to try and give us the
works from above. The more noise the better. Everything you've got. Okay?"

"Okay," said Ruys, "but give me time to get organ-
ized."

"Two minutes enough?"

"Two minutes. We'll be ready."

Goutard turned to me. "We'll leave one to guard the truck. That had better be Musa. We'll go in in the usual way. Grenade first, then yourself." He chuckled. "Wasn't it Ruys who said there wouldn't be any of this sort of fighting?"

"Yes. But we'd better be careful, hadn't we?"

"Careful?"

"I've got Willens' IOU. Didn't he give you one, too? We want to be in a position to cash them, don't we?"

He hesitated but not for long. "It's us or them now."

"I sent Willens' signal."

"You didn't have to. But what's the difference now? That was only insurance. You said so yourself. We don't need insurance any more."

"We don't?" I could hardly believe my ears.

"What for? We're going to win. Come on. Let's get moving."

We got out and he began filling his haversack with grenades. Spare Uzi magazines went into each of his hip pockets. I did what he did automatically. It was as if I no longer had a mind of my own. I really don't remember exactly what happened for the next few minutes. I know that I had a terrible desire to go to the lavatory and that it became hard to think of anything else. I heard Goutard issuing orders to Sergeant Musa and saw him looking at his watch. Then I was marching behind him along the mildewed wall below the barred windows of the Prefecture. We were near the portico when he stopped. I almost bumped into him. He had his Uzi slung over his shoulder and a grenade in each hand. He was pulling the pins out with his teeth.

I saw him toss the two grenades into the portico, step back quickly and flatten himself against the wall. The blast of the double explosion was like a punch in the head. Through the singing in my ears I could hear MAG fire coming from the river front. It was drowned suddenly by the snarl of a Uzi as Goutard ran forward into the portico, firing as he went.

I followed. For some reason it seemed safer to follow than to stay there in the street.

Through a cloud of dust I saw that one of the double doors was open and I heard Goutard yelling at me to come on. Nobody was firing at us. I yelled at the two *macaques* behind me to follow and went in.

There was a reception hall with a desk and chair in the middle and a stairway. I had no time then to see more. Goutard was already halfway up the stairs, taking them two at a time and howling like a fiend. The *macaques* had started howling too. They were right behind me with their bayonets fixed. I had no choice but to run up the stairs ahead of them.

At the top there was a long corridor running right and left parallel with the front of the building. Goutard had turned right—that is, toward the river-front end. As I turned to follow, the noise of the MAG firing outside was added to by the sound of shots fired inside and quite close. At the same moment Goutard pulled out another grenade, threw it to the far end of the corridor and dived sideways through a doorway.

The grenade landed below a shuttered window and when it exploded it blew the shutters open.

I was still standing there dazed from the blast when a

man in a white short-sleeved shirt stumbled into the light from the window. He had a rifle in his hands.

The instant he saw me he dropped the rifle and put his hands up. Then the plaster dust started him coughing.

"Okay, okay," he croaked between coughs. "*Kamerad*, chum, *Kamerad*. *Guerre finie*. We don't want trouble."

I recognized his voice. It was the radio operator who had received Willens' signal.

Goutard charged past him into the end room. A moment later more men in white short-sleeved shirts began to file out of the end room. They hesitated when they saw me. I was terrified, and because I was terrified I suppose I held my Uzi as if I were ready and eager to use it.

Goutard came from behind them.

"That's it, Arthur," he said. "You take charge here. Check all the other rooms. If anyone tries to get funny, cut his balls off. I'm going to give Ruys and Barrière a hand."

Then he left.

I was on my own.

6.

I have been accused of a lot of things in my time and a few of those accusations have been true. I make no bones about that; I don't pretend to be a saint. But the charge that in the Prefecture at Amari I was guilty of looting is absolutely false. There can be no guilt without guilty intent. The worst that I can be accused of is forgetfulness.

Goutard had told me to take charge there and "check all the other rooms." That is exactly what I did. I obeyed orders.

First I told the two *macaques* to collect the rifles and shotguns from the end room. Then I sent the prisoners back to it and told the *macaques* to guard them.

After that I was free to check the other rooms.

The first one I came to, fortunately, was a lavatory. I had a use for that. Then I went on. The rest of the rooms on that floor were all offices and, except for one, rather small and dirty.

The exception was the Prefect's own office, which was in the center at the head of the stairs. This was quite large, with an uneven polished floor and a square of ratty carpet under the desk in the middle. It had two doors, one giving onto the corridor and the other connecting it with the office occupied by the Prefect's *adjoint*.

It was in the *adjoint*'s office that I found the safe.

There was nothing special or imposing about it. It was just an office safe, rather an old one, of the kind that burglars are supposed to be able to open with a bent paper clip.

Naturally, I tried the handle to see if it was locked. Incredibly it wasn't. The *adjoint* had evidently been in such a hurry to leave that he had forgotten to lock it.

Naturally, too, I looked to see what was inside.

The upper half had a shelf for account books. Below were some pigeonholes and a drawer.

I opened the drawer first and saw what looked like a lot of money there. I say "looked like" because, of course, I didn't trouble to count it. Then something in one of the pigeonholes caught my eye. It was a bundle of passports.

There were sixteen of them and they were held together by an elastic band. Slipped under the band on the top passport, a West German one, was a slip of paper with *UMAD* printed on it in red ink. Beside the passports there was a stack of cards, also held together by a band, which turned out to be *cartes d'identité* issued by the Prefect in the name of the Republic of Ugazi for use by resident aliens. It was obvious what had happened. UMAD had made an application *en bloc* for the cards on behalf of sixteen of its employees. The cards and passports were now waiting to be picked up.

Nobody knows better than I what a valuable document a passport is. To leave sixteen passports about where they might be stolen or mislaid seemed to me an absolutely criminal thing to do.

I did what I thought was the right thing.

First I searched the office very carefully to see if the *adjoint*, who had been in too much of a hurry to lock his safe, had also left his keys behind. If he had left the keys I would, of course, have locked the safe and handed over the keys to some properly constituted authority, when one again existed.

As it was, I could find no keys.

Under the circumstances it seemed to me that the passports and the money would be safer in my haversack.

So that is where they went.

Then I forgot about them. And quite understandably, I think. When you are fighting for your life you are apt to forget trivialities.

7.

Kinck and the main body entered the town soon after four. The garrison formally surrendered an hour later. Their heavy machine guns were taken from them and they were confined to barracks pending a truce with the Ugazi government.

After that things went pretty much as Goutard had predicted.

That evening a *macaque* colonel, representing the Emir

of Kundi, arrived with a bunch of thugs from the Fort
Grebanier palace guard and commandeered the hotel.
He also assumed command of the troops and of the
company transport. The European officers promptly
moved into the Prefecture, bringing their MAGs and
mortars and Uzis with them. The UMAD personnel,
both Europeans and *évolués,* who had surrendered decided to stay with us, and three more of their people,
who had been thrown out of the hotel, arrived later. So
did the wounded Barrière and the doctor. Now that the
battle was over everybody in the town was getting
drunk and the place had become even more dangerous
than it had been earlier. The UMAD people weren't exactly friendly, and there were recriminations and angry
talk at first; but they couldn't afford to be too unfriendly, and when someone remembered that there were
several cases of gin in the UMAD offices across the
square, an armed party of both sides was formed to liber-
ate them. They helped to compensate for the fact that,
since there was no kitchen in the Prefecture, we had to
eat our food cold out of the cans.

I had little stomach for food anyway. The reaction
had set in. My legs had given out completely and I
couldn't stop trembling inside. I had an awful desire to
laugh, but knew that, if I let myself do so, I would end up
crying instead. It was a ghastly sensation and I really
needed that gin.

Even so, I couldn't relax completely. Goutard might
not be interested in insurance any more; but then he
hadn't stuck his neck out the way I had. I felt that I still

had to keep my wits about me. And my God I was right.

From the cool look Willens had given me when he turned up at the Prefecture it was obvious that he and Captain Velay had managed to get together and compare notes. Clearly, Willens now knew the time at which I had transmitted his signal. However, he couldn't know for certain that I had purposely delayed it. Although he might not be too pleased with my performance—I wasn't fool enough to think that he was going to honor his IOU —as long as he believed that I had done the best I could, I still had a foot, or at least a toe, in the enemy camp. For a while that was a comforting thought, though not completely reassuring.

Then, suddenly, there were no longer any comforting thoughts, only nightmare.

What happened was Goutard's fault entirely, although that bloody radio operator certainly helped.

There was no electricity in Amari that night and most of the Prefecture was in darkness. We had a few oil lamps, and these were used mainly to light the council chamber on the ground floor. That was where the gin was and so that was where everybody tended to congregate.

It was about ten-thirty when the blow fell.

There had been some shooting in the square outside and nearly everyone had quieted down for a moment to listen. Two of the company officers were on watch by the entrance, and Troppmann and Velay had gone out to find out what was going on.

One of those who hadn't quieted down was Goutard.

He was having an argument with the radio operator and he went on at the top of his voice.

"You don't know what you're talking about," he was yelling. "If you need good luck in this game you'd better not play. Fire power and speed, that's all that matters. If you need luck, you're asking God to kiss your arse for you. Nobody kissed our arses today and don't you think it. We . . ."

He broke off and threw up his hands. He had been speaking in his slangy Marseille-accented French and the radio operator's blank stare had suddenly made him realize that he wasn't making himself completely understood.

"You tell him, Arthur," he said. "Tell the imbecile in English."

I had become too used to obeying Goutard to stop doing so then, but as soon as I started to speak I knew that I had made a mistake. Until that moment I had meant nothing in particular to the radio operator. I was just the man with a gun to whom he had happened to surrender. Now he was hearing me speak English. His eyes widened as he recognized my voice, then narrowed vindictively. He didn't wait for me to finish.

"Oh," he said loudly. "So you're the bastard I talked to on the air this morning."

Kinck, Ruys and Willens were all sitting within earshot. Ruys had actually been listening to the argument. I was almost sure that Kinck understood English. I knew that Ruys did.

Goutard was prodding me in the arm. "What did he

say? What did he say?"

Ruys was looking at me oddly. "The question is what did he mean?" he said in English.

The radio operator was a small, narrow-headed, hollow-cheeked man, and he was quite drunk. If he hadn't been drunk he might have had the sense to shut up at that point, but he didn't.

He pointed at me belligerently. "*He* knows what I mean. Telling me to go bugger myself. Rude bastard. Ask him."

I knew Willens was listening. Out of the corner of my eye I saw him stand up. I hoped he was going to intervene. Instead he moved away casually as if he were going to get himself another drink.

Goutard, who hadn't understood a word, of course, was still prodding me, but I ignored him. It was the radio operator who frightened me now.

"I don't know what you're talking about," I said and managed to smile.

"Are you calling me a liar?" he demanded. "I know a voice when I hear it." Suddenly he imitated my voice. " 'You've got the bloody message. The rest's up to you.' Bastard!"

I knew that there was nothing I could say or do to stop him now. He was the sort of stupid drunk who could go on and on until he had spilled all the beans. Captain Velay, his boss, might have shut him up, but Velay wasn't there. All I could do was to get out of there before things got worse and Kinck started asking him questions.

I stood up and smiled down at him. "Anyone can make a mistake," I said; "but right now I've got to get rid of some of this gin. We'll talk about it when I get back."

He said "bastard" again as I made my way out, but I took no notice. I could feel Kinck's eyes on me. All I wanted to do was to reach the darkness of the entrance hall.

Nobody came after me. The hunt would start later when I didn't return, when the questions had been asked and answered and suspicion had turned into certainty. I had a few minutes in which to think of a way out.

My camp bed and the rest of my things were in one of the offices along the ground-floor corridor. I had to use my flashlight to find my way back to it. I still had no idea of what I was going to do. The command truck was in the compound behind the Prefecture and I had the ignition key. If I could get to the truck I could maybe drive away. But where to? The machine gun had been removed and with the streets the way they were I would be lucky to get out of Amari safely. And supposing I *were* lucky, then what? Back along the river road to Matata and Sikafu? Where then? To Fort Grebanier, where I could perhaps get a plane? That would take hours—hours in which Kinck could radio ahead and have me stopped if he wanted to. Then what? If I weren't hacked to pieces by the *macaques* I would be in jail charged with stealing a SMMAC truck. That would probably be Kinck's way of punishing me. I didn't like to think about what would be done to me if I stayed. Troppmann wouldn't hesitate to put a bullet through my head, nor would Ruys; and there were other more unpleasant things that could happen first.

It was terribly hard to think. I was so tired. I knew that I should be doing something, making a move, instead of just sitting there on my bed in the darkness; but I couldn't seem to bring myself to it. I was terrified and knew that I *had* to escape; but all I *wanted* to do was to lie down on the bed and go to sleep.

There was a small sound at the door and suddenly a blinding light shone in my face.

My stomach contracted and the gin I had swallowed came back sour and choking into my throat.

Then the light moved and I saw that Willens was standing in the doorway. He had his haversack slung on one shoulder and his Uzi on the other.

"Get your things, Arthur," he said. "It's time for us to go."

Part Six

Disengagement

One

I stared at him stupidly.

"Come on," he repeated. "You don't want to stay here, do you? This party's liable to get rough for you and me."

"I know."

"Then let's not hang about. Where's your truck?"

"In the compound."

"Is the radio still in it?"

"Yes. It's padlocked."

"Do you have the key?"

"Yes."

"Then come on."

I picked up my haversack and started toward the door.

"Don't forget your gun. You may need it."

I went back for the Uzi and then followed him out along the corridor.

The Prefecture compound was a small walled area behind the building. Part of it was a garden; but there was a gate on the river-front side and the compound had evidently been used mainly as a parking place. There were two iron-roofed shelters, one with a bicycle rack and the other with spaces for two cars.

I remembered that I had left the command truck in the car shelter. What I also now remembered was that I had parked first and that the four group trucks had been driven in behind me.

I caught up with Willens as we reached the rear door leading to the compound.

"It's no use," I said. "I can't get my truck out. The others are all in the way."

"Don't talk" was all he said. He didn't even pause.

We were in the compound now. Nothing movable and worth stealing had been left in the trucks, so there was no guard on them. There was some yelling still going on in the square, but in the compound it became a distant sound.

"Where is it?" Willens asked.

"On the left. Right up in the corner."

He threaded his way between the trucks, his flashlight probing ahead.

"All I'm interested in is the radio," he said over his shoulder. "With any luck we won't need a truck. If we're out of luck and we do need one, we'll take one of the others."

We had reached the command truck now, and he vaulted into the back of it.

"Where's the key?"

I passed him up the key to the padlock and he went to work. A few moments later the motor generator began to whine in its box.

It seemed as if the whole world must hear it.

"Christ," he muttered, "what a din."

It was too good a chance for me to miss.

"That was why I couldn't send your signal earlier," I said, "because of the noise."

"Well, that's ancient history now." His hands had been busy with the switches. He began to call. "Janson Three, Fielder calling Janson Three, Fielder calling Janson Three. Over."

Janson Two had been UMAD Amari—and that sod of an operator who was talking his head off inside. I had no idea who Janson Three was. I didn't care at that moment. All I wanted was to get out of there before Janson Two blew me completely.

Willens had to call twice before he got an answer.

"Janson Three answering, Fielder. Good to hear you. Over."

The voice was slightly guttural.

That was all I understood of the conversation. Willens began to speak now in a language I had never heard before and was answered in the same language. It sounded a little like Dutch and I think it must have been Afrikaans. After the first few exchanges Janson Three did most of the talking. Willens seemed to be receiving instructions of some sort. It went on and on.

Then I heard Willens say "over and out" and the whine of the motor generator suddenly died away.

"Come on," he said to me. "We won't need a truck, but we have quite a way to walk."

He was already moving away between the trucks toward the compound gate. I started to follow him. To get to the gate we had to pass the back door of the Prefecture. As Willens drew level with it, someone opened it and came out with a flashlight.

Willens was in the open there and the light caught him. He stopped.

I stopped, too, but I was a few paces back hidden by a truck. I couldn't see who was holding the light, only hear.

For a moment there was silence, then the man with the light said, "Well, well!" and sniggered.

It was Goutard.

Willens said nothing.

"Where is he? Is he here?" The light flicked around.

"Who are you talking about?" Willens asked.

"Little Arthur, of course. Who else? Kinck wants to see him. Your radio operator's been talking. Now they want to hear Arthur talk."

"If they can find him."

"Oh, they'll find him. One of us'll find the fat fool. He'll be somewhere in a corner wetting himself. He won't get far."

"Doesn't that worry you, Goutard?"

"Me?" Goutard sniggered again. "What can that *macaque* say about me that they'd believe? I burned the note you gave me hours ago. I was never even near the radio set. *You*'d be the one to worry, I'd say."

He had moved closer to Willens now, and I began to back away behind the truck.

"I'm not worrying," Willens said, "I'm leaving."

"What's it worth to me to let you leave?"

"How do you think you're going to stop me?"

"By going inside and raising the alarm." His light flicked contemptuously at the Uzi in Willens' hands. "You can't use that thing. The noise would bring them running quicker than I would. How much money have you got? How much cash?"

"Nothing you'd want. I left most of it with my wife."

There was a slight pause. When Goutard spoke again the tone of his voice had changed. His temper had begun to go.

"Better think again, Willens. Strictly speaking, you already owe me a thousand dollars. I'll take half of that in francs. For the spot you're in it's a bargain. A bargain," he repeated.

In my mind's eye I could see his face taking on that pinched look.

"Be reasonable," Willens was saying. "I don't have that much money on me."

"Aaah!" There was the gargling noise. I knew that any moment now he would lose all control and that would be the end for me.

I had moved right around the truck by now, so I was very nearly behind him.

"Don't give me that shit," he snapped. "Out with the money!"

Then I could see them both, Willens in front of the truck facing me, Goutard with his back to me jabbing his flashlight at Willens' face.

"Out with it!" he was yapping. "Out with it!"

I was absolutely desperate. There was only one thing I could do to shut him up. I unslung the Uzi, took three quick steps forward and brought the gun down as hard as I could on his head.

He had heard me before I got to him and swung around. But although he saw me, he wasn't quick enough to stop me. The Uzi weighs four kilos and I used all my strength.

He sprawled forward onto his knees. Then Willens kicked him and he went down all the way.

I stood there gaping; I couldn't believe that it had actually happened.

"Quick," snapped Willens. "Help me get him behind the truck."

We took an arm each and dragged him between two trucks where he wouldn't be seen by anyone making a casual inspection of the compound. Then we made for the gateway.

The gates were bolted on the inside, but there was no lock. A few seconds later we were on the river front and walking quickly south, away from the square. Ahead of us there was the glow of a fire.

"Where are we going?" I asked.

"Across the river, if we can make it. They're sending a launch for us from Changa."

"Is that where Janson Three is?"

"Yes. They'll pick us up at a point outside the Amari perimeter. All we have to do now is get there. The last thing Kinck did before he handed over was to move our group down to the river front. If we run into a patrol we'll have to bluff our way through. With any luck, though, they'll be too drunk to stop us."

Most of them were, but we had a couple of nasty moments.

The worst was when we had to get past the fire. It was a river-front warehouse and I suppose the patrols had been looting it earlier. The blaze lit up the whole area, and though we kept as far away as we could there wasn't much cover and no way of making a wide detour. We could see them capering about in the roadway like lunatics and firing their rifles into the burning building. Then one of them saw us and yelled to the others.

Some of them turned immediately and began firing their rifles at us. These were troops who a few hours earlier had been ours. I don't know whether they recognized us or not. Possibly not. They were ready by then to fire at anything that moved.

Willens gave them a burst from his Uzi and then we ran for it. He didn't hit any of them. The burst was just to let them hear the sound of an automatic weapon. They knew that sound and didn't try to come after us.

The next lot we saw had a *macaque* officer with them and weren't as drunk as the others. They had set up a barrier of oil drums across the road and had a cooking fire going on the riverbank. This was near the place where the logs, when they had been trucked down from the hills, were transferred to barges. Off to the right there was a concrete pier with a big crane on it.

The officer peered at us blearily as we approached, and

two of his men made threatening movements with their bayonets.

Willens took no notice of them. He kept his eyes on the officer.

"Everything all right?" he demanded brusquely in his bad French.

The officer hesitated. Willens kept moving.

"Good," he said. "The commandant will be here shortly to inspect your post."

The officer actually returned Willens' casual salute as we marched on.

We were outside the Amari perimeter.

We kept going for about half a kilometer. The road was uphill now and then began to bear away from the river. This was the road the logging trucks came down, and if we had continued along it we would have come to the main road intersection by the brewery.

Willens stopped and got out his flashlight.

To the right of the road the ground fell away fairly steeply to the riverbank and was covered with slimy-looking undergrowth.

"It's not going to be comfortable," Willens said, "but it's got to be done."

He started down and I followed, slipping and sliding on my backside, catching my feet and clutching blindly at things that tore my hands. A branch whipped my hat off and I didn't attempt to recover it. I could hear Willens cursing and swearing somewhere in front of me. Then he called up to me.

"Hold it! Not too fast or you'll go in the drink."

I grabbed wildly at the branches. My haversack strap got entangled around my neck. And then I was in the drink—up to my knees anyway. What had looked from above like the riverbank was a patch of swamp. It stank to high heaven.

Willens was in it too. He had his flashlight on again and I could see him clambering up onto a rotting tree trunk. As I joined him there he began to flash a signal out across the river.

2.

The launch came eventually, its exhaust bubbling quietly as the man at the wheel tried to maneuver it in to the bank. There was a second man in the bow with a gun.

Willens called to him.

"That you, Jan?"

"Yes. Are you okay?"

"Okay. Don't come any closer. It's solid weed here. We'll make it out to you."

I had the presence of mind to keep my haversack dry as we waded out chest-deep to the launch; but I had no strength left to get myself up into it. Willens and this Jan had to haul me up.

I think I passed out for a while.

I remember the feel of the launch turning and the

sound of the engine revving and then nothing until Willens began punching me in the shoulder.

"Come on, Arthur," he was saying. "Hold up a bit longer. Don't go to sleep yet. We're nearly there."

I opened my eyes.

The launch was going fast, jolting across the swift midriver current toward a row of lights on the far shore.

"Changa?" I asked.

"Changa." He reached up and unpinned the Republic of Mahindi's badge from his shirt. "We're in Ugazi now," he said. "Better get rid of these baubles. We won't be needing them any more."

I took mine off, too, but I didn't throw it away. I put it in my pocket. You never know when things like that may be useful. Besides, it was after all an officer's badge.

The lights came closer and the launch changed direction slightly.

"What about these?" I pointed to the Uzis.

"We'd better leave them in the boat." I saw him grin. "Lucky I reminded you to bring one along. It came in handy."

That was all the thanks I got for saving him from Goutard.

I didn't much mind. As my father used to say, "*When a man says he's grateful to you, watch out. The bugger means to come again another day.*"

The real point was that "little Arthur," the white *macaque*, the "fat fool," had *not* been "somewhere in a corner wetting himself" when the moment of decision came. He had been there with a gun and the guts to use it.

Now the Old Man of the Sea had a sore head and Sinbad was free again.

3.

I spent a week at the hotel in Changa.

The town was full of Ugazi troops and more seemed to arrive every day. Some had automatic weapons, and there were even a few armored troop carriers. But nothing happened there to change the situation. There was neither a truce nor a transfer of prisoners of the kind Kinck had envisioned. The Amari garrison remained in its barracks and the other Ugazi forces stayed on their own side of the river. As Velay had predicted, SMMAC's barge traffic out of Matendo had been stopped by the Ugazis. Two of the barges had been sunk by gunfire and a tug had been damaged. After that the barges stayed in Matendo, and the ore trucks from Kawaida ceased to run. Ugazi and Mahindi had both protested to the United Nations Security Council. It looked like a stalemate.

Willens had arranged for UMAD to pay my hotel expenses but I still had his IOU. When I had reminded him of the fact he had said airily that nothing could be settled about that until the whole situation had been clarified.

I took this to mean that if UMAD won after all I might possibly get paid, but that if SMMAC held on to what they'd grabbed I certainly would not.

At first he couldn't be bothered with me at all. He was too busy trying to get his wife back. I don't know exactly how he managed it, but I have an idea. One or two news-agency reporters had turned up in Changa, and I think he got word to Kinck that if she were not permitted to rejoin him immediately, he would give the newsmen the whole story in detail. For SMMAC, highly sensitive to public opinion at that moment and working overtime to come out of the affair smelling of roses, that would have been a serious threat.

Whatever the strings were that he pulled, they worked. Barbara Willens arrived three days later. She had traveled via Zone B, the evacuation of which, she reported, had still to be completed.

It was from her, toward the end of the week, that I had the little lesson in business ethics which may have changed my whole life.

Her husband had gone up to the capital for a conference and we were sitting on the hotel verandah having a drink. It was the first time I had been alone with her since that night in the staging-area camp.

"I'm sorry things didn't quite work out as planned, Arthur," she said.

"I did the best I could, Mrs. Willens."

"So Adrian tells me. Pity it wasn't good enough."

I thought that pretty cool. After all, she'd been the one who had promised that I would be sitting pretty.

"A great pity," I said dryly. "If I'd done less or if I'd done nothing at all, I'd be on the winning side now."

"For what it would be worth, yes." She smiled pleasantly. "You haven't often been a winner, have you, Arthur?"

What a question to ask a man!

"I've survived."

She seemed amused. "Yes, I suppose that's a win of sorts. But if it's any consolation to you, you haven't lost much this time."

"Only my job with SMMAC."

"You wouldn't have had that for long anyway. You know what's going to happen here, don't you?"

"Ugazi and Mahindi will fight it out presumably."

She shook her head. "No. There's nothing more to fight about. The game's over. UMAD and SMMAC have come to an agreement."

"An agreement!" I thought she was joking.

"It may take a while to work out the details in Geneva, but otherwise it's a foregone conclusion. That little patch of rare earth will be mined as a joint venture. Ugazi and Mahindi will share the royalties. UMAD will get a piece of SMMAC's cassiterite operation to compensate them."

"But what about the Ugazi government?"

"Who cares about the Ugazi government? They lost one small slice of territory and gained another. Who's going to reverse that situation? The Ugazi armed forces? They can't. The United Nations? Forget it. The International Court at the Hague? There's been a boundary dispute involving mineral deposits going on between

Venezuela and what used to be British Guiana for over fifty years. The International Court hasn't settled that. This one won't last fifty days. And for a very simple reason. SMMAC and UMAD have decided it won't."

"What right have they to decide?" After all that I'd been through, the idea of those bastards calmly sitting down in an office in Geneva to divvy up the loot really made my blood boil.

"Who else is there?"

"That rare earth belongs to the Ugazis. It's been stolen from them."

She sighed patiently. "We're talking about businessmen, Arthur, not boy scouts. UMAD had something that SMMAC wanted a piece of. So SMMAC made a kind of take-over bid which worked. So now they've got their piece and they're well satisfied. The Ugazis may grumble at first, but when they start drawing their share of the royalties they'll be satisfied, too. What's wrong with that?"

"Nothing, Mrs. Willens," I said stiffly. "It would be a good defense of daylight robbery also."

She laughed. "You're a moralist, Arthur," she said. "How about ordering another drink?"

I have been called plenty of things in my time, but never a moralist before. I wasn't sure that I liked it. It made me feel a bit silly.

4.

It is a strange thing with me. When I have been made to feel silly by a woman, especially a sexy-looking woman, I start thinking really seriously and making plans. I don't mean plans for getting back at her, but plans for getting back at the world and bettering myself.

Curiously enough it was that bundle of passports I happened to have in my haversack that gave me the big idea.

I had been asking myself some questions.

For instance: if I pinch a wallet in a washroom, that's stealing and everyone yells blue murder; but if SMMAC or UMAD pinches two hundred million dollars' worth of rare earth, that's "acquiring an interest" and nobody says a word. Why?

How do they get away with it?

How could I get away with something like it?

I wasn't thinking of anything on the same scale, of course—millions don't interest me—but something that a man with my sort of know-how could tackle without having the police breathing down his neck all the time.

At first I had seen the passports simply as a potential source of income. Naturally, I had considered returning them to Amari, but there seemed no obvious way to do so. Besides, I knew that the UMAD people concerned could easily get their consuls to issue them new ones. I wasn't victimizing anyone.

It was the feel and texture of the passports I had, all sixteen of them together, that made me think of them in terms of capital rather than just income.

Basically they were all much the same—booklets in colored covers with embossed or stamped heraldic designs. Some had elaborate engraving inside and pages that were water-marked and overprinted, but most were fairly simple. Two of them had the name of the printer in small type on the inside of the back cover. It was a firm in Frankfurt, West Germany, though they weren't West German passports.

The idea of forgery didn't enter my mind, of course. People like SMMAC and UMAD get away with things because they stay above or outside the law and because there isn't a policeman who can breathe down *their* necks. If I wanted to get away with something, I would have to follow their example.

What really interested me about those passports, apart from their value on the black market, was that, although they represented six different nationalities, they all looked so much alike. Two of the six in fact were practically the same color.

And then I began to think of all the countries there are in the world with new names—names like Botswana and Lesotho and Malagasy and Rwanda—that most people have never heard of. Give them their old names—Bechuanaland, Basutoland, Madagascar, Ruanda-Urundi—and still a lot of people would be hazy about them.

All these new countries that nobody knows about issue passports. That is one of the things about independent sovereignty—you can issue passports.

I asked myself some more questions.

There are over one hundred and forty sovereign states in the world today. Why shouldn't there be one more sovereign state that nobody has ever heard of? And why shouldn't it issue passports?

What happens when an immigration official examines a passport?

He looks first to see if the picture stuck inside it is vaguely like you. Then he looks to see if it is still valid and up to date. If you're entering a country that needs a visa, he checks that. Lastly, if he's one of those bastards with a black book on the desk beside him he looks you up to see if you're on the list.

But that's all. He doesn't ask you about your country. If you come from Burundi or Bhutan or Malawy or Gabon he doesn't say he's never heard of it and want to know if it belongs to the U.N. He's not interested. You have a passport that seems to be valid. It's his job to stamp it, so he stamps it.

By the time Willens returned from the capital I had everything more or less cut and dried.

"I'm getting tired of sitting around in this bloody place," I told him. "I like a little action. If UMAD'll buy me a plane ticket, I'm prepared to forget about the IOU."

He looked relieved but suspicious.

"A plane ticket to where?"

"Tangier."

He smiled thinly. "Tangier's not so free and easy as it used to be in the good old days, you know. Things have changed since the Moroccans took over."

"It'll do me," I said. "I need a change."

Two days later I left the Republic of Ugazi.

5.

I had been right about Tangier. It hasn't changed all that much. I have been able to sell eleven of the sixteen passports quite easily and for a good price.

Tomorrow I leave for Frankfurt.

I have a mission in life now.

There are still lots of persons in this world who are stateless through no fault of their own. I should know. I want to help them.

The Nansen passport is no more. I believe that a passport-issuing sovereign state created solely and specifically to aid the stateless person in his quest for formal identity and his struggle against the powers that be is long overdue. For obvious reasons the name of it must remain confidential for the present; but in creating such a state I consider that I am performing a service to mankind. If, in years to come the name of Arthur Abdel Simpson is remembered as that of a man who helped the outcasts among his fellow men, then I shall be content.

The current cash price of a Panlibhonco passport in Athens is twelve hundred dollars U.S.

I think that's disgraceful.

The price of my new passport will be only *five* hundred dollars U.S., or the equivalent in any convertible currency.

I think that's fair and reasonable.

Eric Ambler

Eric Ambler was born in London in 1909. Following his graduation from London University, he served an apprenticeship in engineering, toured England in a vaudeville act, wrote songs and, for several years, advertising copy. In the period from 1937 to 1940 Mr. Ambler produced four of his most successful novels: *Background to Danger, Cause for Alarm, A Coffin for Dimitrios* and *Journey into Fear.* He joined the British Army in 1940 and was discharged a lieutenant colonel in 1946, having been in charge of all military training, morale and education films for the Army. After the war Mr. Ambler left off writing novels to write and produce a number of motion pictures for the J. Arthur Rank Organisation. For his screenplay of Nicholas Monsarrat's *The Cruel Sea* he was nominated for an Academy Award. In 1951, *Judgment on Deltchev*, his first novel in eleven years, was published. This was followed by *The Schirmer Inheritance* (1953), *State of Siege* (1956), *Passage of Arms* (1960), *The Light of Day* (1963) and *A Kind of Anger* (1964). Mr. Ambler is also the editor of *To Catch a Spy: An Anthology of Favorite Spy Stories* (1965).